"Sam, what did the shaman say?"

"He says you're a bossy woman who talks too much, but he admires your spirit."

"I can live with that," Noel conceded. "Did he say I can take my equipment into the interior?"

"Yes, but there's a catch." Sam studied her before going on. "Despite your mighty spirit, you're still a daughter of Eve. He can't let your strong woman's influence taint the sacred grounds. So he wants to dilute your feminine power. You'll have to be . . . cleansed."

"No problem," she said, her shoulders straightening in growing confidence. "I believe in honoring the local customs. So what does he want me to do?"

He rubbed his chin. "You're not gonna like it."

"I don't have to like it, Sam," she said smoothly. "I've got a mission to accomplish, and I'll do whatever it takes to get into the sacred mountains. What does he want me to do?"

"Not you. Us." He bent so close to her ear she could feel the heat of his breath rush through her body. "He wants us to get married."

WHAT ARE *LOVESWEPT* ROMANCES?

They are stories of true romance and touching emotion. We believe those two very important ingredients are constants in our highly sensual and very believable stories in the LOVE-SWEPT line. Our goal is to give you, the reader, stories of consistently high quality that may sometimes make you laugh, sometimes make you cry, but are always fresh and creative and contain many delightful surprises within their pages.

Most romance fans read an enormous number of books. Those they truly love, they keep. Others may be traded with friends and soon forgotten. We hope that each LOVESWEPT romance will be a treasure—a "keeper." We will always try to publish

LOVE STORIES YOU'LL NEVER FORGET
BY AUTHORS YOU'LL ALWAYS REMEMBER

The Editors

786

AND BABIES MAKE FOUR

RUTH OWEN

BANTAM BOOKS
NEW YORK · TORONTO · LONDON · SYDNEY · AUCKLAND

AND BABIES MAKE FOUR
A Bantam Book / May 1996

ISBN 0-553-44517-0

Published simultaneously in the United States and Canada

Bantam Books are published by Bantam Books, a division of Bantam Doubleday
Dell Publishing Group, Inc. Its trademark, consisting of the words "Bantam
Books" and the portrayal of a rooster, is Registered in U.S. Patent and Trade-
mark Office and in other countries. Marca Registrada. Bantam Books, 1540
Broadway, New York, New York 10036.

PRINTED IN THE UNITED STATES OF AMERICA

OPM   0 9 8 7 6 5 4 3 2 1

DEDICATION

To Connie Canright, for her endless
energy and unfailing encouragement,

and to Geralyn Williams, for her
sympathetic ear and voodoo prayers.

ONE

Paradise isn't all it's cracked up to be, Dr. Noel Revere thought as she shielded her eyes from the high-noon sun and watched the chartered plane climb into the clouds. She saw the flash of its silver wings, signaling its irrevocable departure. She lowered her hand and sighed. There goes finger sandwiches, *The Wall Street Journal*, little bottles of liquor. . . .

She swept her gaze earthward and looked around the strip of cleared ground known optimistically as the St. Michelle International Airport. The entire complex consisted of the "runway," a tattered wind sock, and a dilapidated hangar that hadn't seen a repair since World War II. The only soul in sight was an almost immobile man sitting on a three-legged stool near the hangar's open door, lazily swatting flies. Once again she glanced heavenward, pulling at the high collar of her fashionable, but stiflingly hot, Dior blouse. There goes TV, air-conditioning, indoor plumbing, civilization. . . .

"Hell," she grumbled as the speck of the plane vanished from sight. But, hell or not, she was stuck with the situation. She'd taken on the assignment after Dr. Bob Harvey, Sheffield Industries' original choice for this project, had sprained his ankle in a Little League softball game. Personally, Noel thought it was highly suspicious that Bob had tripped over the pint-sized first baseman right after he learned just how primitive the island's accommodations really were.

The last time Boston-bred Noel had braved the wilderness she'd been eleven—she'd spent two days at a Girl Scout jamboree and the next week in bed recovering from a nasty case of diarrhea and poison oak. Her idea of "roughing it" was a Holiday Inn, but she'd agreed to take Harvey's place at the request of her boss and best friend, Katrina Sheffield-Fagen. Make that her *former* best friend. Best friends didn't talk you into leaving your air-conditioned Miami condominium to spend ten days on a cloyingly humid, practically deserted Caribbean island, researching a theory that had as much chance of panning out as proving the moon was made of green cheese—

Beep.

The small, plaintive sound came from a pile of baggage and computer hardware sitting beside her on the sunbaked runway. Guiltily, she realized she wasn't the only one feeling the heat. *Poor babies. Their circuits must be frying. Dammit, where is that guide Sheffield hired? He was supposed to meet the plane.*

She wiped her dark, sweat-damp bangs from her frown-creased forehead, thinking wistfully of her luxury condominium just north of Miami, with its cabanas and Olympic-sized swimming pool. If she hadn't let herself get talked into this assignment she could be there now, sitting by the pool sipping a frozen strawberry daiquiri with Hayward and her other friends. Now *that* was paradise. But she couldn't afford wishful thinking—not with Einstein and PINK baking like Maine lobsters in the West Indies sun. She gave the jumble of equipment a gentle pat, then hurried off toward the hangar and the only living soul at this sorry excuse for an airport.

She went up to the man sitting beside the hangar's entrance. "Excuse me, have you seen a guide named Sam Donovan? He was supposed to meet me here."

The old man glanced indifferently in her direction. His face was as worn and weathered as a piece of old leather, ugly beyond belief, but his dark eyes sparkled with the keenness of a star-studded night. They wrapped her with a subtle magic, making her think of cool trade winds, lazy mornings that lasted all day, and rosy sunsets that slid gradually into soft indigo nights. The slow pace of paradise unsettled her to the depths of her industrious Puritan soul.

Apparently it didn't unsettle the old man one bit. He turned away without a word and went back to swatting flies.

I guess I can take that as a no. "Well then, could you

help me with my computers? I've got to get them out of the sun before their circuits are damaged." She reached into her purse and pulled out her wallet, extracting first a ten, and then a twenty. "I'll pay you. See? American dollars."

She waved the bills under his nose, as if the odor could attract him. She was offering a princely sum, and his threadbare shirt and loose, patched pants showed that he could clearly use the money. But the man didn't even glance at the bills. Instead he ignored her, continuing his leisurely task of batting flies—apparently finding them only slightly more annoying than he did her.

Noel's jaw tightened. Her reserved and socially prominent grandmother had trained her to keep the temper she'd inherited from her Italian father in check, but the sun and sweat had melted away much of that hard-learned restraint. "Look, mister, I'm not asking for the world—just a few minutes of your time. If thirty dollars isn't enough, I'll pay more. What the hell do you want?"

"It's just a guess," a deep voice behind her commented, "but I think he's looking for a 'please.'"

Noel spun around in alarm, an alarm that increased as her gaze slammed into a pair of the bluest, fiercest eyes she'd ever seen. Hurricanes and tidal waves were in those eyes—the violence that was the flip side of paradise. Instinctively she stepped back, pulling her own eyes away from the overwhelming power of his gaze. She caught a brief impression of hard, unforgiving features, a strong chin covered by several days' worth of stubble, and shaggy hair streaked gold by the sun. He looked like the kind of man who'd kill her for thirty dollars. He looked like the kind of man who'd kill her for thirty cents.

And he was naked to the waist.

He smelled like sweat and sun, untamed and unmastered. She swallowed, feeling helpless in more ways than she could name as she tried to ignore the muscular expanse of his tanned, fur-dusted chest. Her sensible New England soul rang warning bells of alarm. *I'm virtually alone in the middle of nowhere with a half-naked criminal and a small fortune in computer equipment.*

"What, in God's blue heaven, made you wear that getup?"

A half-naked, fashion-conscious criminal. "I . . . it's my favorite."

"Not in this climate," he stated in a voice as rough as new-made whiskey. "Not for long, anyway."

He gave her a thorough once-over, as if he meant to steal her clothing as well as her equipment. The thought brought a searing blush to her cheeks, but not necessarily from embarrassment. *It's the heat. It's making me crazy—*

Once again she was distracted by a voice behind her, but this time it came from the old man. The words he spoke were low, melodious, and completely unintelligible, but his dark eyes gleamed with laughter. Puzzled, she turned back to the other man. "What did he—hey, what do you think you're doing?"

While her attention was focused on the old man, the outlaw had walked over and hoisted up several pieces of her heavy, expensive computer equipment as if they were made of plywood. Without even bothering to look in her direction, he strode off toward the far side of the hangar.

"Put those down!"

"Lighten up, sweetheart," he growled without breaking stride. "My Jeep's over here. It's old, but I think it'll carry most of this junk."

Junk? *Sweetheart?* "Look, if you take that equipment, you'll be sorry. It belongs to Sheffield Industries, a major international conglomerate. They'll have Interpol on you in a skinny minute. In fact, they've already hired a local man who's got a background in international security."

"Really?" the man drawled.

"Yes, and he'll be here anytime." Noel hurried after him—not an easy task in stiletto heels and a tight skirt. She prayed that the security man's reputation was as well deserved as Katrina's husband, Jack, a former troubleshooter himself, said it was. "His name's Sam Donovan. You've probably heard of him."

"I've done a hell of a lot more than heard of him, Dr. Revere."

Noel stopped in her tracks. Oh no. It couldn't be. Katrina and Jack had promised her a seasoned guide with a security background, not some scruffy, half-dressed, ill-mannered desperado. She swallowed, watching him load the equipment into a dented, battle-scarred army Jeep. *"You're* Sam Donovan?"

"In the flesh," he replied, not realizing how appropriate the description was. He leaned against the frame, and glanced back at her with his all-too-penetrating blue gaze. "You know, it wouldn't kill you to help with this equipment, even if you are a Ph.D."

He made her title sound like a disease.

"I was going to help." She wished the words didn't sound so defensive. She'd always done more than her fair share of the "grunt work" at the main office, but she wasn't about to waste her breath justifying herself. Instead, she marched over to the pile and grasped the handle of one of the heaviest pieces, starting to lug it toward the Jeep.

He pulled it out of her hand, shouldering the weight as if it were a Tinkertoy. "I said help, not get a hernia. If anything happens to you, Jack will take it out of my hide. Use your head, sweetheart. For both our sakes."

"I'm not your *sweetheart*," she said as her ire rose to match the temperature. It was bad enough having to give up modern comforts for the ten days it would take to complete her assignment, but to spend it in the company of an arrogant, muscle-bound cretin . . . "I don't appreciate being patronized."

"And I don't appreciate—" he began, but stopped as the old man again interrupted him.

"Jolly-mon." He nodded to Donovan. Then he pointed directly at Noel, and said something that he clearly considered a hoot.

Noel was hot, aggravated, and in no mood to be

laughed at in a language she didn't understand. "What did he say?"

Donovan shrugged and set the heavy box on the ground. He pulled a faded bandanna out of his back jeans pocket and used it to mop the sweat at the back of his neck. It was an insignificant motion, but it drew Noel's attention like a magnet. She couldn't help noticing how the sun glanced off the bronzed planes of his chest, and how his worn jeans molded to his muscular thighs like a second skin. Hayward wouldn't look like that if he worked out for a decade, she thought, then cringed at the unconscious disloyalty. After all, even though they'd ended their romantic relationship months before, he was still a good friend. *Honestly, Noel, you've never gone in for that stupid macho stuff.*

At least, not until now.

She licked her lips, which suddenly felt bone dry despite the oppressive humidity. "What did he say?"

Donovan gave a dry chuckle. "Trust me. You don't want to know."

Anger built like a thunderhead inside her. This guy was her employee, and the sooner she made that clear, the better. "Look, Mr. Donovan, for the next week and a half I'm paying the bills, so I'm the boss. You do what I say—period. Now tell me what that old man said."

His eyes narrowed and his jaw pulled into a hard, tight line. Once again she sensed the violence within him, straining like a wolf on a chain. A hellishly handsome blue-eyed wolf . . . But this time she sensed something in herself as well—small, twisting and unfamiliar, with an underlying violence that matched his own. She stood rigidly still, frozen by his gaze and the strange, unexpected currents it created inside her. Adrenaline coursed through her, but not from fear. She wished to God it was from fear. . . .

Donovan stuffed his bandanna into his back pocket. "He says you're scrawny as a chicken, and have the disposition of a warthog, but you've got great legs and a tight little ass, and he figures you'd be pretty good in bed." He flashed her a grin as uncivilized as the rest of him. "So tell me, *sweetheart*, any truth in that?"

This is a bad dream, Noel thought as she tightened her grasp on the Jeep's roll bar. In a minute I'm going to wake up in my own apartment, in my own bed—

But as the Jeep roared through another pothole, she was forced to admit the truth. She was careening through the depths of a Caribbean jungle in a vehicle that threatened to rattle apart at any moment, driven by a macho maniac who wouldn't know a safe-driving lesson if it bit him in the a—

Another bone-jarring jolt cut short her imaginings. She cast a worried glance at the equipment in the back of the Jeep, with special concern for the two small notebook PCs perched on top. The ordinary-looking units contained two of the most extraordinary personalities she'd ever known—Sheffield's remarkable artificial-intelligence computers PINK and Einstein. With the technicians' help she'd painstakingly downloaded subsets of their personalities into the PCs, taking duplicates of their programs to help her in her analytical research. Technically the AI computers were still safe and sound in the powerful Sheffield mainframe back in Miami. But for all practical purposes they were being bounced and battered just as badly as she was.

"Can't you slow down?" she asked the man behind the wheel.

Donovan gave a belligerent snort. "This Jeep only goes two speeds—flat out and stop. But relax. I know these roads like the back of my hand."

Yeah, but how long since you've looked at your hand? Donovan inspired many emotions in her. Confidence wasn't one of them. Still, as she stole a clandestine look at his profile, she honestly had to admit that his other attributes were pretty impressive.

Tanned and tough, he was pure muscle from his sinewy arms to his washboard stomach. His rugged profile had none of Hayward's refined handsomeness, yet it drew her eye like a flame draws a moth. Health clubs could have made a mint using him in their advertisements. The man radiated sheer animal power like the sun radiated heat. There was something almost infernally irresistible about the unrepentant strength of his jaw, and the ruthless directness of his shockingly blue eyes. A man's man, she thought, trying to box his image with the cliché. She might have succeeded, if she weren't such a stickler for honesty.

She didn't trust the man. She was well on her way

to detesting him. Yet her research-trained gaze saw the disturbing shadows that haunted his deep-set eyes, and the sensitive, expressive mouth that was so much at odds with the rest of his harsh, frowning features. She looked away, feeling jarred in a way that had nothing to do with the pothole-pocked road they traveled.

Clearing her throat, she steered her thoughts in a safer direction. "How long have you known Jack?"

He shrugged. "Fagen? We worked together on and off for years, handling security and defense projects for emerging nations." He gave her a sharp, sideways glance, as if he knew she expected the worst of him. "I'm qualified to handle the AI prototypes, if that's what you're driving at."

"That's not—" she began, shaking her head in frustration. She'd always considered herself a calm, levelheaded person, but Donovan managed to push every one of her hot buttons. Consistently. If he kept this up she wasn't going to survive a week, much less ten days. "Look, I know we started off on the wrong foot, but we've still got to work together. Can we start over and at least try to be civil to each other?"

Donovan never took his eyes from the road. "Lady, one reason I left the States was to get away from 'civil.'"

Well, I tried, she thought glumly, looking away. It wasn't her fault if this cretin didn't want to be polite, but it was going to be a long ten days. Take it a day at a time, she told herself. In less than two weeks she'd be off this godforsaken island, and back to her regular job, her friends, her climate-controlled condominium.

And to her climate-controlled life.

Lord, where had that thought come from? She had a wonderful life—a challenging job, an elegant condo, lots of friends. What more could a woman want?

More, whispered a contrary inner voice. *Much, much more.*

"You're right," Donovan said suddenly.

Noel whirled to face him, her eyes wide with shock. He couldn't have read her mind. Could he? "Wha-what do you mean?"

"My bad attitude." The tension in his hard jaw eased slightly as he gave her a look that was almost contrite. "Look, I've got nothing against you personally, but until I got Jack's letter this morning I was expecting a man. Sending a woman here . . . well, it complicates things."

Noel's great-grandmother on her mother's side had been an advocate for women's rights, and the doctor stiffened with every ounce of her suffragette heritage. "I can do the research as well as Dr. Harvey. Better, if you want to know the truth."

"I'm sure you can." Donovan flashed her the edge of a disturbingly disarming smile. "I'm just not sure you're going to get the chance. The mountains you plan to explore lie at the heart of St. Michelle, both geographically and spiritually. The islanders won't want a woman—especially a *foreign* woman—treading on their sacred ground."

"But I have permits." She reached down to pat her bulging, soft-side briefcase. "I've got dozens of them—everything from trespassing exceptions to a fishing license. I've been legally approved by every bureau in this country's government."

"Maybe so, sweetheart," Donovan explained with a cynical smile, "but that *government* is two islands and fifty miles of ocean away. Official permits don't mean jack sh—er, squat on St. Michelle. The only law these people live by are the traditional tribal-Catholic-spiritual customs they've adhered to for the last hundred-odd years. And the only recognized authority is the chief shaman, Papa Guinea."

"A shaman? Like a witch doctor?"

"Got it in one," he commented gruffly.

He slowed the Jeep to an almost responsible speed and turned off the main road onto a narrow, green-canopied path. The overgrown lane made the road they'd just left seem like a superhighway, but Noel hardly noticed the new bumps and potholes. She was too busy thinking about the bulging stack of impressive-looking permits in her bag—useless permits if what Donovan said was true. She winced, recalling all the time and trouble she'd spent procuring the documents—all the hours she'd wasted while the island bureaucrats sent her from room to room to room. The officials must have known from the start that the documents would be worthless once she reached the island, but they'd taken her company's money just the same. Bastards, she thought grimly, realizing too late that her country didn't have a lock on dishonest politicians.

All right. If they weren't going to play fair, neither would she. "Couldn't we just sneak into the mountains by the back roads?"

"We could—if we didn't care about having the entire population out for our blood. Don't let the sleepy atmosphere fool you. These people take their religion seriously, and defiling the sacred lands is as good as a death sentence."

She glanced at the man beside her, the only person she'd met who'd told her anything like the truth. She wasn't entirely comfortable with the thought. Actually, she wasn't one bit comfortable with the thought. Depending on Sam Donovan for a ride was bad enough—depending on him for anything more bordered on suicidal. She'd rather have trusted a force-five hurricane than her guide, but she had no choice. The Eden Project was her responsibility, and she needed Donovan's help to get it done.

"All right. If this Papa Guinea is the person I need to see, then you'd better take me to him."

"You don't just waltz up to Papa's door and demand to see him. Not unless you want to spend the rest of your life as a chicken."

"Surely you don't believe in voodoo magic," Noel scoffed.

"I'll give you a free piece of advice," he said in a voice so chilling, it raised the hackles on the back of her neck. "If you want to make it through the next ten days you'll show some respect for 'voodoo magic.'

When you stepped out of the plane you stepped over the line. You're not in the civilized world anymore. The rules are different here."

The rules are different here. She watched the shadows of the overhanging vines slide across the hard contours of his face and body. His expression was closed tighter than a tomb. She suspected he was the kind of man a person could know for years, and not really know at all. The kind of man who could pretend to care about you, then turn around and leave you without even saying good—

"We'll see him," Donovan stated suddenly.

She shook her head, putting aside memories she'd boxed and shut away almost thirty years before. "See who?"

Donovan grimaced. "Papa Guinea, of course. He's holding a general assembly tonight at the old church. If we approach him together, we might be able to convince him that you're harmless. At least, we might convince him—if you keep your mouth shut. Think you can do that for an evening, sweetheart?"

"I'm not your—" Noel began, but her words died in her throat. At that moment the Jeep reached the end of the green-walled path, leaving the close, humid depths of the jungle behind. They came out on a bluff overlooking the island's small but bustling harbor. But as far as Noel was concerned, they'd entered another world.

A cool, salt breeze blew off the water, reviving her, filling her with the rich, secret smells of the ocean. Ships of every size and description wandered across the shining blue meadow of the bay, their seemingly random movements fitting together into a huge, chaotic, yet somehow precise symmetry.

She smiled, charmed beyond words. This was the paradise she'd imagined as a child, the warm, sun-kissed dream that had kept her spirit warm during all those long, sunless winters she'd spent in her grandmother's rigid and joyless household. It was the dream that had kept her child's heart from breaking as she watched her beautiful, once-laughing mother fade away to a pale, lifeless shell. . . .

She was so caught up in the memory that she didn't immediately register that Donovan had pulled the Jeep to a stop. By the time she did, he'd already hopped out of the driver's seat and yanked two heavy cases from the open back. She turned, noticing the low, Mediterranean-style bungalow perched like an elegant bird on the bluff's edge, shaded by immense, ancient banyan trees. "This looks a little small for a hotel."

"That's because it isn't one," he grunted as he hoisted one of the cases on his broad shoulder. "There aren't any hotels on St. Michelle. No tourist trade. Visitors, when we get them, stay in private homes. You'll have to stay here."

An uneasy suspicion formed in her mind. "Where's *here?*"

He readjusted the case, and gave a curt nod in the direction of the nearest banyan tree. She glanced toward it and caught sight of a weathered wooden sign hanging from the lowest branch, swinging gently in the lazy harbor breeze. The white lettering was sun-faded but still legible. S. DONOVAN. Her gaze whipped back to her guide, who stood staring at the sign with an expression as glum as her own.

"Like I said, sweetheart," he told her grimly. "Things would have been a hell of a lot less complicated if you'd been a man."

From: e.stein1@corp.sheffld.com
Received: from relay1.sheffld.com by mail05.mail.remote.com
To: p.pink1@corp.sheffld.com
Subject: EDEN PROJECT
Text: *Hey Babe, what's shakin'? Did you catch the drift on voodoo witch doctors and sacred lands? We might be on the right frequency after all. Einstein out.*

From: p.pink1@corp.sheffld.com
Received: from relay2.sheffld.com by mail07.mail.remote.com
To: e.stein1@corp.sheffld.com
Subject: EDEN PROJECT
Text: *Voodoo-schmoodoo. Check out the doc's blood pressure when she looks at Donovan. There's more going on here than meets the super VGA monitor. Lay you odds we'll have our equation solved before I can bet the trifecta at Hialeah! PINK out.*

TWO

God had ten commandments. Sam Donovan had three. Never drink alone. Never cheat a friend. And never, ever do business with a woman.

He'd already broken two of them.

He'd broken number one when he'd gotten Jack Fagen's letter—delivered only a week late because it was stamped *Urgent*—informing him that Dr. Harvey was being replaced by a Dr. Noel Revere. Cursing, Sam had poured himself a shot of straight tequila, and tossed it back in a single gulp.

He'd broken commandment number three when he'd reached the airfield, and watched the crew from the charter plane unload the doctor's equipment— and the doctor. Surprised, he watched the slim, dark-haired figure walk with remarkable dignity down the rickety steel steps. He hadn't expected one of Sheffield's top computer scientists to be so young. Or to be wearing a sweat-drenched silk shirt that hugged her very unscientific curves like a fast car on a slick track.

He'd had plenty of opportunity to flag down the pilot—to explain that this whole trip was a waste and that the lady should head back where she came from. But he hadn't. Instead, he'd stood in the shadows of the hangar, studying her like a moray eel studies a passing angelfish. She'd lifted her chin and marched across the field, her petite build at odds with her determined expression. Wrong fish, he'd thought as a rare smile tugged at his lips. She's more like a blowfish—a tiny terror that swells to twice its size when it's riled.

On the drive to his bungalow he'd discovered just how accurate that description had been—the lady was about as angelic as a lighted stick of dynamite. Still, Sheffield Industries was paying him a great deal of money for playing tour guide to her and her equipment—a cake job. He didn't know what she was researching and—beyond the fact that it wouldn't hurt the ecosystem of the island—he didn't much care. The good doctor could have all the secrets she wanted—as long as Sheffield Industries paid him cold, hard cash. Hell, for enough money he could even overlook the fact that she was a woman.

But as he pushed open the door to the bedroom that had recently been his, and saw a black silk stocking draped over the end of his carved mahogany four-poster, he silently admitted that overlooking her sex was going to be a hell of a lot tougher than he thought.

He stopped, listening to make sure that the shower at the end of the hall was still going strong. Then he headed across the bedroom toward his closet, bristling with territorial ire at the feminine clutter draping his once inviolate domain. Hell, the place was even starting to smell like a boudoir! And the worst part of all was that it was his own damn fault. He could have given her the lumpy living-room couch. She was expecting it—when she realized the bungalow had only one bedroom she'd headed toward the living room without a single word of complaint. That's when he'd spoken up like some overaged Boy Scout, blurting out that she could use his room.

That soft heart will get you into more trouble than a dog has fleas.

The gravel-voiced memory brought a ghost of a smile to Donovan's lips. Uncle Gus. Damn, he hadn't thought of that sharp-eyed old reprobate's favorite saying in years, not since—

Donovan stiffened, his smile hardening into a tight, bitter line. Ruthlessly, he shoved Uncle Gus's memory aside, just as he'd locked away all the memories of his former life. He didn't want to deal with his past. And here, in the lazy, languid world of St. Michelle, he'd found he didn't have to.

He opened the closet door and reached into the dark interior, to the back corner where he kept his most prized possession—his tackle box. Fishing was the closest thing Sam had to a religion, and he did his best thinking while he was casting line. He intended to spend the next hour in well-deserved solitude on the rock jetty below his bungalow, deciding how best to present the doctor's case to Papa Guinea. It wouldn't be easy since the island's views on women were right out of the Middle Ages. Still, getting her access to the sacred grounds was part of his job. The other was keeping her undeniably shapely little rear end out of trouble until—

His thoughts ended abruptly as his fingers closed, not on the metallic hardness of the tackle box, but on a mass of soft, silky material. Jerking back his arm, he extracted a handful of frilly feminine underwear. "What the hell is this!"

"Garters and camisoles," a helpful nearby voice replied. "Victoria's Secret's Spring Sale. Excellent buy."

Donovan started. He glanced around, assuring himself that he was the only one in the room. Yet someone had spoken, and the tinny voice definitely didn't belong to the doc. "Who said that?"

"I did, dude," the voice replied, this time accompanied by a short, mechanical whir. "What's shakin'?"

The whir gave the speaker away. Processing chips. Following the sound, Sam glanced over at the ironwork table near his bedroom's wide French doors. Currently, the antique table was piled high with very modern computer equipment, which gleamed like newly minted coins in the slanting rays of the afternoon sun.

In the midst of the scattered equipment were a couple of notebook PCs and multimedia speakers,

surmounted by an ultralight camcorder on a small tripod stand. As he watched, the camcorder slanted
forty-five degrees to the side, in a strangely human
simulation of a person cocking his head.

Sam moved closer, his anger momentarily overrid-
den by wonder. "Einstein?"

The camcorder jerked up and down. "That's my
name. Don't wear it out. And you're Sam Donovan,
the 'Lucky Irish.' "

Sam rubbed his chin. "You know about that nickname?"

"Sure do. And I know about Syria, and the assassi-
nation plot in Germany, and saving the dozen people
in—"

"Okay, I believe you." Sam had forgotten the
computer had access to all his records. *All* his records,
he thought as a frown creased his forehead. The last
thing he wanted was to have his self-righteous em-
ployer find out about the months following his stint in
the army—months he'd spent the last two years trying
to forget. "Let's just keep my past between the two of
us. Still, I guess you'd better call me Sam, considering
how much you know about me."

"Sure thing. Pleased to meet ya, Sam, and so's
PINK. Aren't you, babe?"

"Charmed," agreed a higher-pitched voice from a
speaker on the far side of the table. "You're the cat's
pajamas."

"Thanks, I think," Sam answered. Fagen had sent
him material on the prototypes' technical features,
but he hadn't warned him that they were quite so,

well, human. He peered at the equipment and took another step closer, intrigued. *It's been a long time since anything's made me this curious.*

Not that long. He glanced down at the frilly and delicate underthings still clutched in his fist, and thought about their leggy, brainy, and completely perplexing owner. She'd been a puzzle right from the start. The lady had the body of a centerfold and enough letters after her name to start her own alphabet, but her mouth seemed permanently fixed in a frown. He'd never seen a mouth more in need of a smile. Or a kiss.

PINK's camcorder spun in a tight arc, focusing on his chest. "Interesting. You don't look the least bit dirty."

He looked down, giving himself a quick scan. His jeans were a little dusty from the trip, but that was all. "Why should I be d—"

"And you don't look beastly, either," PINK continued, rotating her cam toward Einstein. "He doesn't resemble a filthy beast. Noel's mistaken."

Sam's jaw tightened dangerously. "She called me a filthy beast?"

" 'Filthy, hulking, oversexed, macho-jerk beast' were her exact words, I believe," Einstein supplied helpfully. "Maybe she needs her eyes examined."

"For starters," Sam growled, his former compassion dissolving. Several descriptive words for Noel Revere came to mind, none of them repeatable. For now. "Look, all I want is my tackle box. Where'd she put it?"

"Under the bed," E replied. "She said it smelled like fish."

"Of course it smells like fish!" He hunkered down beside the bed, dumping the undergarments in a heap on the edge of the covers. Sheffield Industries isn't paying me enough, he thought as he inched his large frame under the cramped space beneath his bed. Not nearly enough.

He spotted his tackle box shoved into the far corner next to the headboard. With a grunt of triumph he scooted completely under the bed and grabbed the handle, pulling it toward him. Okay, so maybe it did smell like fish. Badly. But that still didn't give her the right to rearrange his things. Or to call him—what was it?—a filthy, hulking, oversexed, macho-jerk beast.

He'd met her kind before. Hell, one of the reasons he'd left the States was to get away from people like her. Self-righteous harpies who wouldn't know a charitable thought if it bit them in the behind. Since she'd arrived the lady hadn't had one good thing to say about him—or about St. Michelle. And Sam, who owed the island and its inhabitants more than he could ever repay, took that as a personal insult.

Two years earlier he'd drifted into the harbor, as scarred and battered as a piece of tide-tossed drift-wood. Working as a mechanic on a ship with a mostly legal cargo, he'd joined his crewmates in a hurricane of a bender—and had ended up alone and nursing a force-five hangover in the local jail. When he got out he'd found that his ship had sailed without him, leaving him stranded and virtually penniless, with only the clothes on his back to his name.

But fickle Lady Luck hadn't deserted him. To his surprise, the simple, goodhearted townsfolk had taken him in like one of their own. He was a complete stranger—they hadn't even known his name—yet they'd generously shared their meager wealth with him as if they'd been richer than Rockefeller. They'd taught him a way of living between the sea and the sky, between the storms of rage and calms of despair that still occasionally battered his soul. *They taught me how to live in the eye of the hurricane. And if I don't move too far in any direction, I can just manage to survive*—

The sound of an opening door curtailed his thoughts. Sam heard Dr. Revere's voice. "Hi, E. Hi, PINK."

He froze. Dammit, she wasn't supposed to be finished so soon. And once she'd finished she was supposed to spend a solid ten minutes primping. The women he'd known always primped after showers. Damn, it was just like her to mess up his plans by doing something unexpect—

Sam's internal monologue screeched to a halt as Noel walked to the bed and dropped her bath towel to the tile floor inches from Sam's nose. His mattress-limited perspective cut off everything above her ankles. Unfortunately, that left him with an unobstructed view of her slim, provocatively arched feet, her toenails painted a ridiculously frivolous hot pink, her light, graceful step, and the undeniable knowledge that she was standing above him as naked as the day she was born.

The vivid image hit him in the gut with the force of the falling walls of Jericho.

He gritted his teeth, wondering how he was going to get out of this mess. He knew she'd never believe his innocent reason for being under the bed. Hell, *he* wouldn't have believed it. She'd accuse him before he got two words out, probably adding voyeur to his list of faults. Filthy beast voyeur, he thought grimly. One step above ax murderer.

Uncle Gus had said he had a soft heart, but no one had ever accused him of having a soft head. He was about to spend ten days in close quarters with this woman—ten days that would be difficult enough without her thinking of him as some sort of pervert. He gripped the handle of his tackle box and shoved his big body farther under the bed, shutting his eyes against the unexpectedly charming and—though he'd have died before admitting it—incredibly arousing image of her slim bare feet with their pink-painted nails. *Hell, maybe I am a pervert. . . .*

He kept his mouth shut, and hoped to hell that the "intelligent" computers had brains enough to keep theirs shut, too.

"So you don't think the diode corrosion will be a problem?" Noel stood beside the bed and adjusted the collar of her white oxford button-down shirt.

"No way," Einstein replied confidently. "And if it

is, we'll just get Sam to take a look. 'Cording to his files, the dude can fix anything."

"Except his manners," Noel muttered, then winced. It wasn't like her to be so mean-spirited—in fact, she was usually the last to say a condemning word about anyone. She ran her hand through her still-damp hair, silently admitting that Sam Donovan had an amazing knack for bringing out the worst in her. She didn't know why. She wasn't sure she *wanted* to know why.

She couldn't deny that he was good-looking. She also couldn't deny that he had a certain animal magnetism about him that she found marginally appealing. But what of it? she thought with a nonchalant shrug. If she took away that macho, muscle-bound physique what did he have left? Nothing. Well, almost nothing. Just those incredible, heart-stopping, breath-robbing blue eyes, and that slow sultry smile that made her insides sizzle like a strip steak on a Texas grill . . .

"So where is our host?" she asked abruptly. "I haven't seen or heard him since I got out of the shower."

PINK piped up. "That's 'cause he's under the—"

"Weather," Einstein interrupted. "Er, the dude wasn't feeling so hot, so he took off for a while."

PINK's camera tilted questioningly to the side. "No, he didn't. He's—"

Suddenly Noel heard the loud whir of Einstein's coprocessor, a sign that he was exchanging a flood of info-bytes with PINK over their coax-cable link.

What kind of information was so critical that he couldn't wait for PINK to finish her sentence? Frowning, she left the bed and walked toward the computers, smelling a digital rat. "Okay, you two, what's going on here?"

"Nothing," E assured her.

"Nothing," PINK echoed. "Sam's not here. He's never been here. And he's not hiding under the bed, either."

Noel glanced sharply at the large four-poster, a horrible thought crossing her mind. What if he— But no . . . Donovan wasn't the type to hide in a dark corner like a Peeping Tom. The man was all bellow and bluster, but somehow she knew he'd never take advantage of a woman. Of course, that didn't make an ounce of difference in the way she felt about him.

And how exactly do you feel about him? her conscience nagged.

Noel bent down, smoothing an almost invisible wrinkle out of her sensible, knee-length navy skirt. "PINK, I think you need to run a diagnostic on your humor program. Your jokes are getting a little thin. Meanwhile I'm going to see if I can locate the absent Mr. Donovan. He said we'd need to meet this Papa Guinea character tonight. I don't intend to miss that meeting—even if our guide doesn't seem to give a damn about his paying clients."

She thought she heard a sharp hiss. Turning, she looked around . . . but it was only the wind rustling through the palm leaves on the terrace. Except for the prototypes, she was alone in the room. Except for the prototypes—and her annoyingly persistent conscience.

Shrugging off her thoughts, she went to the French doors and stepped out on the stone veranda that circled the bungalow. She was determined to set her mind on finding her missing host—until she caught sight of the ocean below. The sun hung low over the western horizon, turning the sea to liquid gold. Brilliant purple bougainvillea and flame-colored birds of paradise poured their blossoms over the stone railing, filling the cooling air with a scent as rich and heady as the finest perfume.

Noel stood transfixed, overwhelmed by the exotic sights, smells, and sounds of the Caribbean evening. Her usually sober restraint melted like winter snow in the incandescent glory of the sunset. She breathed in the darkening air, feeling something fiery and passionate fill her soul.

And how exactly do you feel about Donovan?

She shook her head, as if she could physically shake away the uncomfortable and pointless question. In two weeks this exotic island would be nothing more than a memory—a memory of gold-stained seas, fiery flowers, and of a blond giant who stirred her deep inside. She wrapped her arms protectively around her middle, feeling every inch of the miles between her and Miami. Suddenly ten days seemed an awfully long time. . . .

Her thoughts ended abruptly as a slight scraping sound behind her caught her attention. She turned, discovering that the sound came from her room.

Honestly, those computers were worse than rowdy kids, she thought as she walked back to the French doors, wondering what the two electronic hooligans were up to. "Okay, guys, what's going on—"

She stopped dead in her tracks. Twilight filled the room, but there was still more than enough light to show her the dark shape struggling out from under the bed. Her bed. In her room. The room where she'd been . . . where he'd seen her . . .

Rage, embarrassment, and—oddly—disappointment boiled up inside her. The Italian temper she'd spent her life denying erupted from her core like a seething volcano. She barreled into the room, finally knowing the answer to her conscience's annoying question.

She knew exactly how she felt about the despicable Sam Donovan. And she intended to tell him. In detail.

To: p.pink1@corp.sheffld.com
Subject: EDEN PROJECT
Text: *Batten down the hatches, babe. There's a storm front coming! E out.*

THREE

"You bastard!"

Damn, Sam thought as he turned to face the French doors—and his furious client. So much for a clean getaway. "Look, this isn't what you—"

"How dare you?" she demanded as she tore into the room. She stopped in front of him, her nose inches from his breastbone, looking mad enough to stare down a tidal wave. "How the *hell* dare you?"

Sam rubbed his beard-roughened chin, feeling way out of his depth. He'd spent most of his youth on the water and could navigate the shoals and shallows of the island channels like any sailor born, but he hadn't the first clue about how to steer clear of this lady. Bereft of ideas, he tried the truth. "You've got it wrong. I only wanted my fishing gear. Anyway, I could only see your ankles—"

"And that makes it all right?"

"Yes. No." He shoved his fingers through his hair. "Listen, you've got this all wrong. I wasn't—"

His explanation ended abruptly as she hauled off and socked him on the arm. His battle-toughened hide barely registered the blow, but the courage that drove it impressed him.

Until she hit him again. Harder.

To hell with this. Making a battlefield decision, Sam released his gear, letting the steel box clatter to the floor. The loud sound momentarily distracted his assailant, enabling him to capture her wrists, and hold them effortlessly out of punching range. "Stop it. Just calm down and listen—"

She kicked him in the shin.

Now, *that* hurt. Cursing, he yanked her against his chest. "You want to play rough?" he asked with lethal softness, increasing the pressure on her wrists until she winced. "Because believe me, I can make it as rough as you want."

He expected her to back down, or to dissolve into feminine tears. Instead, she raised her chin, glaring at him, eyes sparking with emerald fire. "If you were only getting your tackle box, why didn't you speak up?"

"Because I knew you'd make a big deal of this. I knew you'd be unreasonable."

"You spy on me while I'm dressing and *I'm* being unreasonable?" she sputtered. "Well, I've got news for you, Mr. Donovan. You haven't begun to see how unreasonable I can be!"

She pulled back her leg, apparently aiming for a

higher location than his shin. Sam bit out a colorful curse, wondering what ancient island god he'd angered to deserve this little wildcat. Probably all of them, he thought as he deftly pushed her off balance and toppled her backward onto the bed. He easily pinned her down with his heavier body. "Sweetheart, I wouldn't tick me off if I were you."

"I'm not your *sweetheart*," she hissed through clenched teeth as she struggled to get free.

A reluctant smile tugged at Sam's mouth. The lady had guts. She was outgunned, outweighed, and outmaneuvered, but she wasn't giving an inch. In another time and place he might have appreciated her courage. But two hours before their meeting with the island's most powerful shaman wasn't the time. And pinned under him while trying to inflict semipermanent damage on vulnerable parts of his anatomy was definitely not the place.

"You're whatever the hell I say you are," he stated in a take-no-prisoners tone. "Let me give you a dose of reality. St. Michelle isn't some tame little Paradise Island. It's a port of call for some of the most ruthless characters ever to sail the Caribbean—and that includes the pirates. People who wander down to the waterfront at night don't always live to see the morning sun. This is a tough, dangerous place for landlubbers who don't know their way around. And sweetheart, you—with your tourist attitude and expensive computer hardware—fit that description in spades."

She stopped struggling. Her eyes still burned with

the white-hot flame of distrust and suspicion, but at least she was listening. Relaxing his grip slightly, he continued. "The only thing standing between you and that pack of cutthroats is yours truly. So unless you want to end up as fish food I'd suggest you cut me some slack. Believe me, on this island I'm your best friend. Your only friend."

She said nothing, but he knew his words had hit home. The icy sheet of anger melted from her eyes, revealing a well as deep as the azure sea outside his window. They were a surprise to him, those eyes. He'd figured that the one thing in the world he understood completely was a woman like her—a stiff-backed, spoiled snob who measured the worth of everything by the dent it made in her American Express Card. But those eyes told a different story. There was a passionate, vulnerable woman hiding beneath her porcupine exterior. *Her soft, warm and achingly seductive porcupine exterior.*

Suddenly he was aware of the delicacy of her wrists, the smell of soap on her newly washed hair, and the fluttering beat of her heart against the wall of his chest. Her starched clothes would have done a nun justice, but the curves pressed intimately against him reminded him more of a cathouse than a convent. She was . . . sweet, he thought, the word evoking an all-but-forgotten tenderness in him. He'd had so little sweetness in his life. Not since Gina . . .

His mind shied away from the memory, but not the sensation. He was a passionate man in every sense of the word, but he'd never been more aware of the difference between sexual need and a deeper, keener hunger. He'd have given ten years of his life to stay like this, breathing in the scent of her hair and skin, lingering over the feel of her yielding body under his. He'd have given another ten to kiss a smile from her uncertain, much-too-serious lips.

"So what happens now?" she asked softly.

He knew exactly what he wanted to happen now—in graphic detail. *This is nuts.* He had no use for women like her, and she thought he was a filthy beast. Yet his mind conjured up a photo spread so graphic that even *Playboy* wouldn't have published it. Blood thundered in his veins. He stared down into her fathomless eyes, feeling something huge and primal shift inside him. Tempted beyond endurance, he brushed his rough finger across the delicate line of her cheek. *Say something, dammit. Anything.* "I—"

"Talk louder," Einstein's modulated voice requested. "We can't hear you."

Sam's head shot up. Both E's and PINK's video cameras were pointed directly at the bed, apparently watching the scene with great interest. "Just what do you think you're doing?"

"Studying human mating behavior," PINK replied with electronic innocence.

"Mating?" he repeated, a rare chuckle rising in his throat. He turned back toward Noel, but she'd slid out from under him with a magician's grace, leaving him empty-handed and feeling strangely, unaccountably, betrayed.

"We were *not* mating," she stated as she hurried to the equipment table. "We were . . . not."

E's camera lens swiveled from Noel, to Sam, then back to Noel again. "You sure? Body position, increased breathing levels, and decreased vocal volume suggest a seventy-two-percent probability of sexual foreplay, leading to—"

"Yes, I'm sure!" she interrupted, her back going poker stiff. "Anyway, it's bedtime for you two. We've got to conserve your batteries. Power down."

The computers' simultaneous "awww" dwindled out as their power-supply lights faded to darkness. In a few moments Sam and Noel were alone again, without their electronic audience. Somehow, that only seemed to make things more awkward.

Noel fiddled with a dial on the now inactive computers. "I'll wipe their databases," she promised without turning around. "Tomorrow morning when they power up they won't remember the last few minutes."

"What about *your* database?" Sam asked gruffly.

She spun around, her eyes burning with fury and her cheeks burning with embarrassment. "Don't flatter yourself. Nothing happened. And even if it did, it doesn't matter. I'm only going to be here for ten days. We have a business arrangement, Mr. Donovan. I think it would be wise to keep it that way."

Wise? he thought. Maybe. Probably. But wise didn't count for much when compared with the feel of her under him—and to the fierce, sweet fire that still burned in his gut. She stood several feet away from him, but he was aware of her every move, her every breath. Energy flowed between them like a powerful undertow, unseen, yet strong enough to drag a man to his doom. Or his salvation. He stroked back his bright hair, watching her intently, hungrily. "It's not that simple. Something just happened between us, something unbelievably powerful. Can you deny it, Noel?"

It was the first time he'd used her given name, and the shock of it brought her hand to her throat. For a moment he saw a flash of the sensuous, vulnerable woman she tried so hard to hide. Then she pulled her shoulders up in a rigidly correct posture, and her eyes frosted over like a secluded forest pond covered by a layer of winter ice—still beautiful, but cold, so very cold. . . .

"Nice try, Donovan. I suppose that line works on most of your clients."

He stood up slowly, until he towered over her. "It wasn't a line," he told her in a voice so bitter, it made hers sound like a balmy island breeze. "But if it were, I wouldn't waste it on an old-maid scientist with ice water in her veins."

He spun away before she could answer, grabbing his tackle box like a consolation trophy as he stalked out of the room. He'd meant to hurt her. She was everything he despised, everything he hated about the "civilized" world that was so unforgiving to the people who didn't fit. He'd watched that world destroy his generous-hearted, hard-drinking, shrimp-boat captain uncle, whose fierce love for his nephew wasn't enough to convince social services to let the boy stay on his trawler. He'd watched "civilized" Western reporters reduce the suffering people of the warring third worlds he was stationed in to statistics for the nightly news. And finally he'd watched supposed friends turn their backs on him when his fledgling computer security company needed money to survive, though at that point he'd hardly cared, since he'd already lost his only reason for keeping it going.

The civilized world had left him bleeding and battered, and the wounds still ached. It had showed him no mercy—so why should he show any to the uptight scientist who was the embodiment of its cold, judgmental heart? He tightened his fist around the tacklebox handle until his knuckles went white. Any insult he'd given her was more than justified by her sharp tongue and patronizing attitude. Then he recalled his last sight of her, how she'd winced at his "old maid" comment as if he'd physically struck her.

He'd meant to hurt her. He just hadn't known it would be that easy.

The trip to Papa Guinea's meeting that night was far from silent. Donovan's Jeep rattled like a complaining old woman as it climbed up the rocky mountain road. Night birds called in the distance, their silhouettes merging into the deep indigo shadows of the dense midnight forest. Horns and bells from the still-busy harbor mingled with the evening noises. The whole night was filled with sound—except for the front seat of Donovan's Jeep. Neither Sam nor Noel had spoken a syllable since the trip started.

Noel shifted uncomfortably in her seat, trying vainly to keep her eyes from straying to the man beside her. He'd changed into loose-fitting pants and an ivory-colored, long-sleeved shirt whose cotton material had been washed to the suppleness of silk. All things considered, his outfit was a great deal less revealing than the one he'd worn last time they'd ridden together, but there was something about the way the soft, well-worn material draped his skin that made Noel feel like she'd swallowed a handful of Mexican jumping beans.

She gripped the Jeep's roll bar, trying to still the turmoil inside of her. She'd have had more luck calming a hurricane. Too clearly she remembered the feel of his body against hers—his heat, his weight, his rich, masculine smell. She recalled the gentle strength of his long-fingered hands, and the way he'd stared down at her, as if he was staring straight into her soul. And she remembered what he'd called her just before he'd left the room. *An old-maid scientist with ice water in her veins.*

Her grip tightened on the roll bar. Of course it didn't matter what he called her—she didn't give a damn what he thought of her. Insulting her was probably his way of compensating for his own deep-seated feelings of inadequacy. Yes, that's it, she thought with a satisfied smile. He felt threatened by her successful career and superior intelligence, so he resorted to adolescent insults to prove his own masculine—

"I'm sorry I called you an old maid," he told her suddenly.

"Wha-at?" she said unsteadily, her neat psychological profile of him crumbling to ruin.

"It was a stupid thing to say," he continued, keeping his gaze firmly on the road ahead. "I was just . . . hell, I don't know what I was. But I shouldn't have said it and I'm sorry."

She stared at him, searching his shadowed face for some hint of scorn or cruelty, but found none. His apology should have calmed her inner uncertainty—instead it made her more confused than ever. She swallowed, aware that she wasn't prepared for him to be mature and compassionate. She wasn't prepared for him to care about her feelings.

She wasn't prepared to like him.

Her troubled thoughts were cut short as he palmed the wheel, turning down a graveled side road. "We're here," he announced.

Looking ahead, she saw a small white building nestled in the indigo shadows of the mountainside. Dozens of torches licked its sides with light, making the old structure blaze like a star in a black velvet sky. The effect was breathtaking. "Why, it's a church!"

"Was," Donovan corrected as he pulled his Jeep into a cleared area beside the building. "The Jesuits abandoned it in the last century, when they consolidated their efforts on the larger islands. A priest still shows up twice a year to perform baptisms and marriages. But it's one of the few buildings on the island large enough to hold a meeting, so Papa uses it the rest of the time."

The Jeep shifted as Donovan got out to walk

around the front, but Noel hardly noticed. She was staring at the strange, exotic, and somehow enchanting structure. The shattered tiles on the roof and the patched and repatched plaster sides told her that the old building had seen better days. Yet the walls had been scrupulously whitewashed, and the eaves and alcoves had been dressed up with dozens of garlands of rainbow flowers. Noel couldn't look away. It jarred something deep within her, something true and elemental, and not altogether tame. Like the deep, wild jungle. Like the warm breezes that poured life into her. Like the flowers, the sea, *Sam*—

"Jolly-mon!"

She looked around and saw a group of torch-bearing islanders waving and smiling at her guide. Despite her anxiety, her mouth pulled into a hesitant smile. "Some of the island's ruthless cutthroats?"

"Okay, so not everyone on St. Michelle is a desperate criminal," Sam admitted as he helped her out of the Jeep.

It was the first time he'd touched her since he'd stalked out of the bedroom. It lasted for only a few seconds, yet the feel of his strong, sure fingers on her bare arm laced through her like ribbons of fire. *Dammit, I'm not supposed to feel this way. Not about him.*

"They called you Jolly-mon," she said in an attempt to redirect her thoughts. "The man at the airport called you that, too. What does it mean?"

"It's from an old island story. Jolly-mon was a wandering storyteller who was loved by man and beast alike. He was captured by pirates and pushed overboard, but the dolphins had heard his stories and wouldn't let him drown. They carried him over the waves on their backs until they set him on the shores of this island."

He sighed, turning his face to the stars. "Papa Guinea gave me that name when I first arrived here two years ago. I'm not sure why—I wasn't very easy to love at the time. I was about as far down as a man can get."

"Why?" she asked before she could stop herself.

Slowly, as if in a dream, he lowered his gaze to meet hers. Torchlight pooled in his eyes, revealing an old pain too deep for healing. For a moment she thought he might open up to her, and it surprised her how much she wanted him to. But at the last instant he looked away, his mouth forming into a hard, self-mocking line.

"It's ancient history, sweetheart. I won't waste your time—or Sheffield's money—talking about it. Now stick close." He started to stride toward the church. "Whether you believe it or not, there are plenty of dangerous characters in this crowd."

He wasn't kidding about the crowd. The entire population of St. Michelle seemed to be packed into the little church, along with some of their livestock. Pigs, goats, and chickens vied with their owners for elbow room, adding their snorts and squeals to the general din. It was an amazing assembly. The place was brighter than day, lit by a thousand candles stuck in almost every nook and alcove of the plaster wall. Figures also decorated the walls, festively painted statues of Catholic saints standing side by side with stone carvings of ancient gods. Noel gawked like a tourist at the gaudy pageantry of the walls until a deep-timbred voice close to her ear whispered, "Careful, sweetheart. If you don't close your mouth one of those hens is gonna make a nest in it."

She stiffened, momentarily disconcerted by the soft warmth of his breath against her ear, and the intimate, irresistible laughter lacing his words. *Irresistible*. She snapped her mouth shut and stepped away, wishing she could step away from her uncertain feelings as easily. "Donovan, I'll thank you to keep your comments to your—"

Her words ended as she plowed into the belly of a large man wearing a Day-Glo-orange shirt. "Oh, excuse me. I'm—"

Ignoring her, the big man yelled over her head to Donovan. "Jolly-mon!"

Smiling broadly, the neon giant pointed to her and chatted to her guide in the lightning island dialect. His smile died as Donovan shook his head and waved him away.

"What was that all about?" she asked as she watched the slump-shouldered giant lumber off through the crowd.

Sam shrugged. "Nothing much. He wanted to buy you."

"He wanted . . . really?" She felt unexpectedly flattered. "How much did he offer?"

Donovan looked at her sharply, apparently surprised by her reaction. Then the edge of his mouth nudged up in one of his rare, sweet, and completely devastating smiles. "Not nearly enough, sweetheart," he murmured.

Their gazes locked. Someone jostled her from behind, but she barely noticed. Donovan's eyes drew her in like a powerful undertow—silent, relentless, seductive, *deadly. I'm here for less than two weeks*, her inner voice warned. *In ten days I'll leave and he'll be out of my life forever. Forever* . . .

"Damn!" he cursed suddenly.

Noel stiffened, bruised by the rough oath during the tender moment. "Well, I'm sorry I troubled—"

"Not you," he answered curtly, nodding toward the other side of the nave. "Them."

She followed his gaze. Two men leaned against the wall, one thin and one burly, but both with the same dark menace in their faces. The thin one rested a mud-booted foot on the head of one of the plaster gods while the big one picked his teeth with a knife. Noel shivered, aware even at this distance that there was something vile about those characters. "Who are they?"

"The Deveraux brothers, Jacques and Emile. Major bad news. Papa kicked them off the island about six months ago, but their mama must have talked him into letting them come back." He gripped Noel's shoulders, turning her to face him. "If one of those guys so much as looks in your direction I want to know about it."

"I'm not completely helpless. I know how to defend myself. Remember this afternoon?"

"I remember us ending up in bed with me on top of you," he answered with ruthless honesty. "You telling me you wanted that to happen?"

"You wish!"

"Like hell. The last thing I need in my life is a stuff-shirted, opinionated—"

"Old maid?" she finished icily.

"That's not—hell!" he breathed, dropping his hands from her shoulders. He rammed his fingers through his hair, changing the neat style into a wildly tousled mane of gold. "Dammit, Noel, you make me crazier than any woman since—"

The stately sound of a bell reverberated through the church, cutting short his speech. A hush fell over the crowd like a dropping cloak. "We'll finish this later," Sam promised in a lethal whisper as he pointed to the raised platform at the front of the nave. "He's here."

Noel balled her hands into fists, fighting down the temper she hadn't known existed in her until a few hours ago. Dammit, the man was insufferable. But she couldn't let herself get involved in his myopic, chauvinist arguments. She had to think of Einstein and PINK, and the Eden Project. . . .

Still fuming, she watched a grandly garbed figure enter the room, wearing an ornate headdress that seemed to be made from the feathers of every kind of bird on the island. He moved with stately, ancient grace toward the thronelike chair at the center of the platform, but when he sat down and faced the crowd she realized she'd been mistaken.

"Why, he's young," she whispered, surprise momentarily overcoming her anger. "He can't be more than twenty."

"Nineteen," Sam corrected. "Age has nothing to do with magical power. Papa was chosen as head shaman by the elders while he was still in his mother's womb."

Her eyes widened. "How could they tell?"

Donovan shook his head. "I've been on this island two years, and I still don't understand half of what goes on. It's a mystical, magical place . . . and sometimes a deadly one," he added, his gaze narrowing as he focused on the Deveraux brothers. "I'm going up to talk with Papa. Stay put. And for God's sake keep out of trouble, sweetheart."

"I'm not your sweet . . ." she began, but her words dwindled off as his broad back disappeared into the milling crowd.

The man irritated her. But she was honest enough to admit that much of that irritation was caused at least in part by an unwanted infatuation. In Einstein's words, the guy "toasted her jets." Well, what of it? she thought, squaring her already rigid shoulders. It was a purely physical attraction—he wasn't her type at all. Revere women didn't fall for macho men with big muscles and small brains. Revere women were above that sort of thing.

But then, other Revere women hadn't met the likes of Sam Donovan.

She watched him step onto the platform and head toward Papa Guinea. There was a coiled restlessness in his walk, like a tiger on the prowl. No, a lion, she amended, her gaze shifting to his tousled gold hair. A proud, sad lion who paces the world like a too small cage . . .

Instantly, she stiffened. *Get real, Noel. Donovan is about as far away from the king of beasts as you can get. He's a glorified beach bum, whose only up there pleading your case because there's money in it for him. He doesn't give a damn about you or your project. He's in it for the money, just like your—*

"*Bonjour*, pretty lady."

She whirled around, and winced as she caught a whiff of stale rum. Her wince turned to real alarm when she found herself staring into the cruel smile of the shorter, built-like-a-tank Deveraux brother.

"*Bonjour*," he repeated, his newly picked teeth gleaming yellow in the candlelight. "I speak English good. I hear you rich, got big-money 'quipment. You come."

He reached out to grab her arm. All he got was air. Noel twisted away and started to push toward the front of the nave. "Donovan! Sam! I need you—"

A loud squeal drowned out her words. Looking down, she saw that she'd stepped on the tender toes of a sow. A large and angry sow. With a large and angry matron for an owner.

The next few minutes were a blur to Noel as she overturned a bushel of oranges, backed into a flapping, crowing rooster, scattered a litter of piglets through the congregation, and tripped over the rear end of a recalcitrant nanny goat. The whole church was in turmoil. Half the crowd was laughing—the other half was yelling for her blood.

"Hell," she cursed as she pulled her bruised body and ego up from the floor. She looked at the dirt-smeared expanse of her designer shirt and the ruined travesty of her hose. So much for making a good impression on the shaman.

Suddenly she was yanked to her feet and dragged unceremoniously to the side of the nave. "Damn, woman! Can't I leave you alone for five minutes without all hell breaking loose?"

"I was trying to get away from a Deveraux. He grabbed me . . . and then there was this pig—" She broke off as a strange, unfamiliar feeling bubbled up inside her. She tried to speak, but her mouth couldn't seem to form the right words. All at once she realized she was grinning. Hugely. Un-Revere-like. "Sam," she said, beginning to giggle, "I stepped on a pig. . . ."

He pulled her against him, muffling her unmannerly laughter against his shirt. He nodded toward his friends in the crowd and gestured toward Noel, making the loco sign. It seemed to satisfy them, and even garnered him a few looks of profound pity.

She was pure trouble, no doubt about it. But her laughter was the brightest thing he'd heard in months—unexpected, unpredictable, and seductive as warm summer rain. It echoed through him, shattering something deep inside him. Unconsciously, he pulled her closer. . . .

Her laughter died. She stiffened and stepped away from his embrace, and began to attempt to brush the dirt from her hopelessly ruined shirt and skirt. She didn't meet his eyes.

"Thank you for rescu—I mean, thank you for helping . . . that is."

"You're welcome," he said harshly.

"Yes, well . . . what did Papa Guinea say?"

She was making for a safe channel. Or so she thought. "He says you're a bossy woman who talks too much, but he admires your spirit."

"I can live with that," Noel conceded. "Did he say I can take my equipment into the interior?"

"Yes, but there's a catch. Despite your mighty spirit, you're still a daughter of Eve. He can't let your strong woman's influence taint the sacred grounds. So he wants to dilute your feminine power. You'll have to be . . . cleansed."

"No problem." Her shoulders straightened in growing confidence. "I believe in honoring the local customs. So what does he want me to do? Sacrifice a chicken or something."

"Not exactly." He rubbed his chin. "You're not gonna like it."

"I don't have to like it," she stated with a pragmatism that would have done her Yankee forefathers proud. "I've got a mission to accomplish—I'll do whatever it takes to get into the sacred mountains. What does he want me to do?"

"Not you. Us." He bent intimately close to her ear. "He wants us to get married."

[Received via Local Area Net, direct cable link]
P-Text: *Psst. E, you didn't power down, did you?*
E-Text: *No way, babe. This island's a jumpin' place at night. Been scanning local ham-radio frequencies for news, information—*
P-Text: *The shopping channel?*
E-Text: [Several nanoseconds pause] *Okay, maybe. Anyway, I surfed into something way cool. Seems there's a wedding going on. Donovan's the groom, and the bride is a foreign devil with a name that means Christmas. Noel!*

FOUR

Sam knew she'd be angry. He just didn't know *how* angry.

Her eyes widened in shock, flashing with the fire of an erupting volcano. "He's kidding. He's *got* to be kidding!"

"Trust me. He's dead serious," Donovan promised grimly. "Papa Guinea won't let an unmarried woman enter the sacred lands. I don't like it any better than you do, but if you'll keep quiet a minute you'll see it's not that bad—"

"Not bad?" Her voice rose with her fury. "A teenage witch doctor orders me to marry a man I barely know, and you say it's not *bad?*"

"Keep it down," he warned, glancing over his shoulder at the curious bystanders. "Some of these folks understand English."

"Great. Then they can translate *this* to your shaman. I think you are the lowest, crudest, most despicable creature who ever crawled out of the slime—"

She got no further. Sam yanked her against him and clamped his hand over her mouth—then almost lost his grip when she struggled and tried to take a chunk out of his hand. *Why me, God? What did I ever do to you to deserve this hellcat?* "Listen, you little . . . you know how much you don't want to marry me? Well, trust me, sweetheart, that goes *triple* for me. But Papa Guinea is a spiritual authority, not a legal one. He *can't* marry people."

Her eyes still blazed with emerald fury, but she stopped struggling. At least she was willing to listen to him. Or was plotting her next assault. He figured he had about three seconds to convince her, if that. Leaning down, he whispered low into her ear so that only she could hear him. "The priests come here every six months—they travel in a circuit around the small islands of this area. But six months is a long time for hot-blooded young couples to wait, so Papa 'marries' them—and the church fathers make it legal on their biannual visits."

She mumbled something unintelligible against his palm. Giving her a look of warning, he pulled his hand away.

"So we wouldn't really be married?" she whispered slowly.

"Not unless you wait around for a priest," he promised. "Use that Ph.D brain of yours. You'd get to do your research. I'd get my money. Everyone's happy."

"Except it's not exactly . . . honest," she said hesitantly.

Great. A hellcat with a conscience. "The only thing honest's gonna get you is a plane ride back to the States. If that's what you want, fine, but . . ." His voice trailed off as he looked at the crowd gathering around them. Apparently others had heard about Papa's judgment and were curious to see what the "crazy foreign woman" had decided. "They're waiting for you to make the call. It's up to you, Noel. What's it gonna be?"

She stared at the crowd, biting her lower lip in indecision. The unconscious gesture robbed the stiffness from her coolly resolute face, revealing the soft, vulnerable woman beneath her rigid exterior. Suddenly Sam found himself wondering about her past, and about what had made her hide her softness below that layer of frosty reserve. It wasn't his business. It wasn't likely to become his business, since she was probably going to be on the next plane out of here. But as his gaze riveted on the innocently seductive motion of her teeth worrying her bottom lip, he found himself wondering all the same. Wondering that, and other things . . .

"Okay," she said quietly as she lifted her gaze to his, "but I'd still rather sacrifice a chicken."

Her joke curled around them like voodoo smoke, wrapping them in an enchantment, drawing a hesitant grin from both their unyielding mouths. The shared smile lasted less than a second, but it jarred something deep and rock solid at his core. *A smile like that could haunt a man's dreams. It could make him wish for things—impossible, crazy things that could rip his heart out if he let them—*

"Hey! Jolly-mon is getting married!"

The laughing, cheering crowd surged against them like sea foam. One second she was in his arms—the next she was being pulled away by a dozen animated women. Noel looked back at him in panic. "Sam?"

"Don't worry. They're just taking you to—" His sentence ended abruptly as Jean Duprey the stonecutter slapped him heartily on the back, driving the air from his lungs.

"You'll need more stamina than that for tonight, Jolly-mon." Jean laughed as he thrust a mug of frothing brew into Sam's hands.

Sam took a taste of the bitter, potent liquor, knowing from experience to stop after a few sips. The drink, known by the innocuous name of "sugar water" had a kick like a rampaging elephant. But he doubted even a barrel of the stuff could quiet the turmoil inside him. Intellectually, he knew that this marriage was just a business partnership, nothing more. They didn't love each other. Hell, they didn't even like each other. In two weeks she'd go back to the States, he'd get an "annulment" from Papa Guinea, and they'd go on with their lives as if nothing had happened.

It's just business, he repeated silently as he lifted the cup to his lips and indulged in a final pull of the powerful, numbing liquor. So why did he feel like

he'd just fallen overboard in the dead center of the
Atlantic?

"Hey . . . don't do . . . cut that . . ." Frustrated,
Noel shut her mouth, realizing that no one was listening. Sighing, she raised her arms, and let the women
who'd brought her to the church's small vestry room
pull off her soiled shirt and skirt. I'm doing this for
science, she reminded herself as the women wadded
her expensive designer clothes into a bundle and
tossed them into the corner. I'm doing this for the
Eden Project. And I'm going to get PINK and Einstein into the central mountains of this island even if
it means getting dragged off by a pack of women who
can't understand me, being stripped down to my underwear, and even getting married to a cretin like
Donovan.

Married to Donovan . . .

She shivered, an electric jolt shooting down her
nearly naked spine. *Get real, Noel. You're not really
marrying the guy.* Yet the thought of marrying Sam
Donovan—even a counterfeit marriage—made her
feel like a pot of water on high boil.

"Mademoiselle?"

Startled out of her thoughts, Noel looked down at
the little girl who stood at her side, and drew in her
breath. The child was beautiful beyond words—not
just because of her face or features, but because of the
love and trust that radiated from her enormous eyes
and brilliant smile.

Her sunburst smile still beaming, she held up a cup of what looked like water. *"Pour vous. De l'eau à sucre."*

Sugar water, Noel translated silently, her high-school French class coming to her rescue. Probably some sort of island bridal tradition—and not a half-bad one considering the humidity and the tension. A cool, sweet drink was just what she needed. "Thanks. I mean, *merci.*"

Nodding, she returned the girl's smile with genuine appreciation and lifted the cup to her lips—and almost gagged. The stuff was wretched—more like a dose of medicine than sugar water. She started to hand it back, when the little girl spoke again.

"Pour vous. Pour l'amour de mon ami Jolly-mon."

For the sweetheart of my friend Jolly-mon. Noel could see the true affection in the girl's eyes—she wasn't just saying this as part of some bridal ritual. Surprised, Noel realized that her "macho-jerk" guide had taken the time and trouble to befriend this child, something she knew Hayward would never have done. She couldn't help admiring him for it—and the thought of liking Donovan on any level scared the living daylights out of her.

Distracted, she took another drink from the cup, and was surprised to find that the second taste wasn't nearly as bad as the first. In fact, she found it rather refreshing. She drained the cup and handed it back to the girl, who quickly replaced it with another. Another tradition, Noel thought as she took a sip of the second cup. *Well, it's not so bad. I could even get to like it.*

The next few minutes were full of hectic activity as the women brought out a length of colorful, silky cloth and began to drape it around her body. They laughed and chatted endlessly in French that was too rapid for Noel to understand. Actually she wasn't sure if she would have been able to follow the conversation. Her mind was caught like a fly in a spiderweb, wound tight with thoughts of men like her former boyfriend Hayward, marriage, and the way her life was supposed to be.

Though she'd broken it off with the workaholic Hayward, she still suspected she'd eventually end up with someone very much like him. A CPA, he'd plotted out their future with an accountant's skill, determining the neighborhoods they'd live in, the friendships they'd cultivate, even the schools their two-point-four children would attend. It was a safe and secure future, as different from her mother's foolish and tragic marriage as night from day. Yet try as she might, Noel couldn't conjure up a picture of her children looking at Hayward with the love and adoration she'd seen in the little girl's eyes when she'd spoken of her "Jolly-mon."

Noel found herself wondering if security was enough. She hadn't really thought about it before. But now, as she took a sip from her third (or was it her fourth?) cup of sugar water, she couldn't seem to think of anything else.

All at once the women stopped talking and stepped away. The sudden, unnatural silence unnerved Noel. She started to speak, but found the words unaccountably hard to form. Thoughts and images began to run together in her mind like a watercolor left in the rain. Yet beneath the confusion was a clarity she'd never experienced before, as if all the muddled everyday concerns of her ordinary life had been swept away, revealing diamonds.

A floor-length mirror appeared in front of her out of what seemed like thin air and the image in the cloudy glass captured her attention—a slim woman with hair as dark as midnight, wrapped in an exotic dress that seemed to be made of spun rainbows. Astonished, she lifted her fingers to touch the cold glass, to prove to herself this was a reflection. Her reflection. *But this can't be me. This strange, exotic woman has nothing in common with Noel Revere, who's about as unremarkable as gray Vermont granite.*

Confused, she looked around for her companions, but they seemed to have evaporated like smoke in the wind. Nothing made sense on this island—from the myriad plaster gods, to the suddenly appearing mirror and the disappearing women, to the exotic customs, the unfathomable laws, the sweet water with the bitter taste, the macho-jerk guide who took time to befriend a child. . . .

Nothing made sense. She swallowed, looking again at the woman in the mirror—a woman who had less in common with her than night did with day. The phantom reflection was exotic and passionate, but not unfamiliar. Memories bubbled to the surface of her mind—a flash of a smile, a mischievous wink, the rich, vibrant sound of a man's deep laughter. She'd kept the memories locked deep down inside her, jailed beneath the conservative constraints of her starched business suits and Puritan demeanor. She'd thought she was free of her painful past, but in the shadows and silence of the little room she could no longer deny the unsettling, unwanted truth.

It was conservative Dr. Noel Revere who stared at the reflection in the dark glass. But it was the ghost of her reckless, unreliable father who stared back at her.

Where the hell was she?

Donovan stood with his foot propped on the lowest altar step, staring at the half-open vestry door. "The others came out five minutes ago," he muttered, his frustration growing by the second. "What's the holdup?"

"Who knows a woman's mind?" answered Jean Duprey in the breezy cadence of the island. A wide, knowing grin creased his face. "Getting anxious, Jolly-mon?"

Yeah, but not in the way you think. Donovan glanced over at his friend, the man who had taken him in his first day on the island. Over the years he'd grown to think of the Dupreys as the family he'd never had, and had recently become godfather to Jean's youngest son. Relying on that friendship again, he'd asked Jean to stand up for him at the wedding. *If* there was going to be a wedding.

As the minutes ticked by, Sam became more and more convinced that Noel had had second thoughts, and that she'd figured that being married to him—even unofficially—was too high a price to pay for her research project. Not that he blamed her. This whole thing was damned unorthodox, and unorthodox didn't come easy to by-the-book types like Dr. Noel Revere. Besides, she'd made it painfully clear that she couldn't stand the sight of him.

Jean slapped him soundly on the back, jarring him back to the present. "You are some lucky fellow. I tell you now that I was worried about you. You been here so long and you take no woman."

Sam gave a short, humorless laugh. There were shortages on the island, but willing companions wasn't one of them. "I haven't exactly been celibate, my friend."

The older man didn't return his smile. "Those women feed the hunger of your body, not your heart. You need more, Jolly-mon. You have for a long time."

You're dead wrong. I don't need anyone, he thought, looking away before his friend saw his cynical, self-deprecating grimace. Sure, there were times when he envied men like Jean, who'd found a good, loving woman to settle down with. But that life wasn't for him. His one sail into the hazardous waters of love had left him alone and stranded on the reef of despair. He'd be a fool to chart a course back into that kind of hell again.

He rubbed his beard-roughened jaw, recalling just enough of the past to make himself remember why he'd left it behind him for the simple, undemanding lifestyle of St. Michelle's "Jolly-mon."

"She's here," Jean whispered.

Finally, he thought, turning back around. Now we can get this charade over wi—

He caught sight of her, and froze.

They'd changed her clothes for the traditional multicolored wedding dress of the island—he'd expected that. But he hadn't expected the way she'd look in it, like a delicate, beautiful angelfish swimming through the night reef of the crowd. Her stiffness was gone, replaced by the subtle, mesmerizing grace he'd seen earlier that day in the bedroom when she'd thought she was alone. Unable to stop himself, his gaze slid down the slim, glove-snug material of her dress, over her barely concealed curves, to the dancing slimness of her bare feet. Dammit, she could have worn her shoes at least. A Ph.D should wear shoes. . . .

Like a swimmer dragged down by a strong current he stepped down off the altar and reached for her hand. She turned at his touch, and looked up at him with eyes deep enough to drown in. The brittle frost was gone, revealing an honesty and strength of spirit so pure it robbed him of his breath. Her trust shattered him. Her beauty intoxicated him. He fell into her gaze, feeling an ache inside him for something more than passion, more than sex. She was fascinating. She was irresistible.

She swayed against him, and gave a small, discreetly refined hiccup.

She was drunk.

"Lord," he groaned, steadying her arm. "How much did you have to drink?"

She blinked, clearly having some trouble focusing. "A few cups. Was only sugar water."

"Yeah, well that *water* could fuel a space shuttle. Just follow my lead, okay?" He grasped her elbow and drew her to his side, and tried to guide her toward the stairs. No luck. She swayed again in his arms, tumbling against him in a way that sent an electric jolt slamming through his already overcharged system. *I can't do this. I can't marry a woman who hates me so much she had to get drunk to do it. Even I'm not that low.*

"Look," he whispered rawly against her ear, "you don't have to do this. I'll take you back to the car."

"But my research . . ."

"We'll find another way."

He stepped down and started to steer her away from the altar. Unexpectedly, she dug her heels into the dirt floor.

"I'm not going," she stated, her delicate jaw set in a stubbornness a mule would have envied. "There *is* no other way. Said so y'self. I've got to do this. Einstein and PINK're depending on me. Can't let them down. Can't be like *him* . . ."

Sam didn't know who *him* was, and now sure wasn't the time and place to ask. Jean was peering at them suspiciously, and even Papa Guinea had looked up from his audience with a member of the crowd. In another minute the shaman would smell a rat and call the wedding off, regardless of what either of them wanted.

And what exactly do you want, Donovan?

He shoved the question away. He could deal with only one crisis at a time, and right now he had all the trouble he needed looking at him with wide, uncertain, and hopelessly innocent emerald eyes. He was a hard man who'd lived a hard life, but her gaze ripped through his tough hide like a rhino bullet through body armor. Christ, the kid didn't have a clue what she did to him with that trusting, almost worshipful look. Or how little he deserved it . . .

Think about the money. He dragged his gaze from hers, forcing his mind onto the job and the money he'd make doing it. That was what mattered. That was real, not some crazy emotion that he had no more business feeling than a pig did sprouting wings. He grimaced, pulling his jaw into a tight, hard line. "Okay, it's your call," he growled as he gripped her elbow and steered her up the steps. "But this is your idea, not mine."

In the candlelight he caught the edge of her green glance, full of gratitude and heartfelt relief. He jerked his gaze away, knowing he didn't deserve that, either.

I'm getting married.

The words buzzed through her head like persistent flies as she knelt in front of the altar rail. She tried to concentrate on the fact that this wasn't a real marriage, and that the feather-garbed shaman per-

forming the ceremony had no more authority to pro-
nounce her someone's wife than the local dogcatcher,
but her mind wouldn't cooperate. Her thoughts kept
straying to the man who knelt beside her at the rail, a
man she barely knew. And what she did know didn't
make her feel very safe.

She glanced over at him. Candlelight shifted over
the rugged planes of his face and illuminated the
sheen of sweat on his tanned skin. He was still as the
stone steps they knelt on, yet she could sense the cold
fire burning inside him, the violence that both frightened and fascinated her. She swallowed, her gaze riveted on his remote expression, feeling a strange
hunger build inside her. No, *safe* wasn't a word anyone would use to describe Sam Donovan. But there
were other words that came to mind, words that
would send her proper New England ancestors spinning in their graves—

She yanked her gaze away, trying to collect her
scattered thoughts. No luck. The soft, sacred cadence
of Papa Guinea's indecipherable words, the staring
interest of the hundred people and the thousand gods,
and the strange, seductive energy she'd felt since she'd
landed on the island wrapped themselves around her
like a second skin. Unable to resist, her gaze crept
back to the man beside her.

Okay, I'm human, she admitted silently as she
stared at his heartbreakingly handsome face. Her gaze
drifted down the strong column of his throat, fasten-
ing on a glistening bead of sweat sliding down his

skin. She bit her lip, fighting an urge to press her mouth to that throat and lose herself in the hot, heady taste of his flesh. She'd always repressed her fantasies, seeing them as part of the bad blood that ran through her very proper veins. But for once she didn't feel guilty. After all, what was the harm in it? He wasn't interested in her physically—he'd made that more than clear with that "old maid" crack. So why not let her imagination live a little? Why not pretend, just a minute or two, that this was a real marriage?

So she pretended. She imagined that she was madly in love with him, and that he was madly in love with her. She visualized him taking her in his arms and kissing her—not the predictable, measured kiss that Hayward gave her, but a kiss as wild and unpredictable as the waves that thundered against the island shore. She closed her eyes, drowning in the lush, forbidden fantasy. But there's no harm in it. No harm at a—

"Oh hell," he muttered.

Noel froze. Had he read her mind? It was impossible, but the impossible seemed an everyday event in this weird, magical place. She cleared her throat, making a titanic effort to keep her voice steady. "What's a matter?"

"Something I forgot, something about the ceremony. I have to kiss you."

"What?"

"Pipe down," he growled, gripping her wrist. "We've come this far. Don't blow it now."

"But a kiss!" Her mind reeled from a harmless

fantasy that had suddenly become dangerously real. If he kissed her he might realize what she'd been fantasizing about. And she'd die if he found out, she'd just die.

He said nothing, but his expression hardened, growing still and deadly. Papa Guinea and the crowd faded to nothing, leaving only the reality of his strong fingers gripping her wrist, his muscular form towering over her like a dark mountain, and his eyes searching hers with a stabbing, subtle violence. His gaze absorbed her, stripped her bare, leaving her vulnerable and exposed, spiritually naked. Too late, she realized that kissing him could cost her more than her pride. It could cost her her soul.

Sobered, she turned away, her prim Boston accent creeping back into her whispered words. "I'm sorry, I simply can't kiss you. You'll have to explain to Papa Guinea that—"

He tightened his iron grip to something just short of pain. "It's not a choice. You can't trash these people's customs just because you think you're better than they are."

"I don't! I—"

"Save it," he hissed. He dropped her wrist and gripped her jaw, turning her face up toward his. "It's showtime, sweetheart. Don't worry, I'll make it quick. I'd rather swim in a shark-infested cove than kiss you."

She opened her mouth to protest, but she never got the chance. With masterful but passionless skill he tilted her head to the side, and lowered his mouth to cover hers.

And all hell broke loose.

    [Received via Local Area InterNet, direct
                cable link]

P-Text: *Dr. Revere getting married? To Donovan? But that doesn't compute. They hate each other.*

E-Text: *Looked like it to me, babe. But we must have missed some essential equation. Maybe it has to do with this sex thing humans are always going on about.*

P-Text: *Oh yeah, that. I'll increase the weight of the variables in the equation. Anyway, it looks like this Eden Project is going to be a lot tougher to calculate than we thought.*

E-Text: *[Two parsecs of electronic sigh]. Darn these carbon-based life-forms—they never behave logically. And I thought this assignment was gonna be a piece of toast.*

FIVE

Sam knew she was expecting a swift, unremarkable kiss. That was exactly what he intended to give her—until she tried to wriggle out of the slight request like a trout off a fisherman's line. Okay, so maybe he wasn't like the well-mannered, well-heeled suits she was probably used to kissing, but he wasn't garbage either. And he'd bet the entire profits from this assignment that he knew a hell of a lot more about kissing than any of her yuppie boyfriends.

In two weeks she probably wouldn't even remember his name—others hadn't. Noel Revere was cut from the same cloth. She'd forget him before the film was developed from her high-resolution, diamond-focus, cost-a-small-fortune camera. But she's not going to forget this kiss, he pledged silently as he lowered his lips to hers. At least, not easily.

He covered her mouth in a consuming embrace, swallowing her small gasp of protest. Her eyes widened in shock. Good. She balled her hands into fists and tried to push away. Better. He stationed an arm strategically against the small of her back, locking her against him. *You can't wriggle out of this one, little fish.*

She glared at him, her icy gaze speeding through surprise, through shock, and ending in burning fury. He grinned against her lips, enjoying the hell out of her anger. He liked her mad, liked the way it took the starch out of her oh-so-proper manner. He deepened his kiss, realizing he was beginning to like a lot of things about her.

She wasn't what he expected. She tasted like wine—warm, bloodred wine that pounded through every part of his body. Her lips may have been pursed in a prim expression, but that was the only thing proper about them. They were a man's worst temptation—hot and erotic, and innocent enough to make a man believe she meant it. He thrust deeper, exploring the secrets of her mouth, taking her with the passion that had been burning in his gut since she stepped out wearing the rainbow dress . . . hell, since she'd stepped off the plane.

His senses blurred, seduced by the fire beneath her ice. She made a small, guttural moan and sank against him, her yielding body melding to his from shoulder to thigh. Her woman's scent mingled with the smell of incense and passion, intoxicating him, driving him full-throttle toward desire. He forgot about the church, Papa Guinea, the money, the farcical wedding—nothing mattered except the fact that she was warm and real and in his arms. It didn't matter why he'd started kissing her. He only knew that kissing her filled up an empty place inside him, a place that hadn't been touched in a long, long time. . . .

I'll kill him! she thought, her face burning with embarrassment as his mouth erotically plundered hers. When this wedding was over she was going to make him pay for this—for pulling her against the length of his rock-hard body, for making her aware of his strength, his heat, his musky masculine scent, and for turning her blood to pure fire with every slow, deliberate stroke of his intimate invasion.

Her forbidden fantasy was a joke compared with reality. Violent emotions ripped through her, creating an ache in deep and secret places. His power roared into her like a tidal wave, crashing through her brittle reserve, shattering her barriers in a single pounding heartbeat. She couldn't breathe. She raised her fists to push him away, but instead found herself twining her arms around his neck. Just another second, then I'll kill him, she promised as she wove her fingers through the thick hair at the base of his neck, pulling him closer. Her rock-solid Puritan morality dissolved like gritty smoke in the hurricane of his passion, making her feel aching and vulnerable, and wildly, shamelessly alive. *It's the sugar water. It's got to be the sugar water.*

But the reason didn't matter. She parted her lips, starving for his caress, aching for a deeper, more wicked embrace. She felt as if another woman had stepped into her skin—the secret sinner she'd kept locked deep inside her since her childhood. All her life she'd walked the straight and narrow. She'd lived her life by rigid standards, afraid that one slip would bring out the reckless, devil side of her nature. Well, she'd slipped all right—big time. Now, wrapped in a virtual stranger's fiery embrace, the woman who'd always done the "right" thing found herself wanting to do the wrong thing. She wanted to be bad—wonderfully, hedonistically, unforgivably bad with Sam Donovan. And she wanted to do it over and over again. . . .

In slow motion Donovan lifted his head and looked down at her with an intensity that left her weak. He stared at her in a kind of confused wonder, like a small boy who's just been presented with an incredible toy that he can't quite figure out how to use. The look cherished her beyond words, and shattered her more completely than his kiss. She stared up at him, every bit as confused as he was. For the first time in her life she felt as if someone was looking at her—at *her*, not a Revere descendant, not her father's daughter. For the first time she felt as if she mattered to someone because of who she was, not what she—

"Jolly-mon!"

The booming voice startled them both. Noel looked up, and met the black, laughing eyes of the man who'd stood beside Donovan during the ceremony.

"Jolly-mon," he cried in battered and broken English. "And Mrs. Jolly-mon. You two big happy. Make big . . ."

He made a gesture that would have sent her well-bred grandmother into a swoon. Noel was less shocked—though she still colored to the roots of her hair. But embarrassment was only a small part of what she felt. She was flushed from the drink and giddy from the kiss, and warm all over from the way Sam had just looked at her. She glanced back at him, smiling shyly.

She met the cold eyes of a stranger.

"You're a hell of an actress," he said grimly as he got to his feet. "Don't let anyone tell you different."

"But I wasn't . . ." Her words dwindled off. Regardless of how it had started, regardless of what he thought, she'd meant that kiss. She believed that with every fiber of her being.

But she was less sure—in fact, she wasn't sure at all—that it had meant anything to him.

The crowd flowed between them, separating them. Music started up in one end of the church, an unwieldy combination of reggae beat and voodoo chant. Noel found herself surrounded by the women she'd met earlier in the vestry. They hugged and coddled her, kissing her cheek and giving her advice she couldn't even begin to understand. Noel nodded, gamely trying to keep up the appearance of happiness for a little longer. But it was a poor appearance at best. Regardless of what Donovan thought, she was no actress.

Outwardly she smiled. But inwardly she felt the same way she had all those years when she was growing up under her grandmother's disapproving eye—

like she was being blamed for a crime she hadn't committed.

The trip home from the old church was, incredibly, even more silent than the trip there had been. Sam sat behind the wheel, his face molded into a frown as dark and somber as the surrounding night. Noel was curled into the far corner of the Jeep's passenger seat, watching the yellow headlight pick up the rutted road ahead, wrapped in her own intensely private thoughts. She should have felt relieved that one of the strangest days in her ordered life was finally drawing to a close. Instead, she had a profound sense of loss and disappointment.

And an even profounder sense of confusion over Donovan's kiss.

She shifted uncomfortably against the Jeep's worn leather cushions and tried with everything in her to forget Donovan's kiss. No luck. The memory lingered not just in her mind but in every part of her body, making her feel tight and achy in outrageously intimate places. She stole a glance at the man beside her, hoping reality would dilute the memories. Worse luck. Moonlight and shadows blurred the harsh lines of his profile, making him appear less cynical and strangely, heartbreakingly alone. And loneliness was something she understood all too well.

Come on, Noel. You ought to be ready to throttle the guy. He's an opportunist. He took advantage of you in a public situation. He had no right to kiss you like that.

And you had no reason to kiss him back.

The call of a hidden bird threaded silver through the night air, but she barely heard it. Instead, she huddled as close to the open side of the cab as she could without risking a fall. A seat belt would have been nice. A clear conscience would have been better. She had loved Hayward. She had even thought she would marry him at one time. And yet she'd returned Donovan's kiss with a hellfire passion she'd never experienced with her ex-boyfriend, not even when they'd made love. . . .

She had to regain her composure. She gripped the roll bar and looked out into the darkness, casting through her mind for something safe and innocuous to say. "Um, how soon can we start out for the mountains, Mr. Donovan?"

"*Mister* Donovan?"

"That's your name, isn't it?"

"Sure, but—" He glanced at her, the moonlight glittering in his eyes like demon fire. "Come on, Noel. We *are* married. Besides, that kiss put us on a first-name basis."

"I'd prefer it if you didn't mention the marriage— or the kiss—again," she stated, her voice as rigid as her posture.

He shrugged and turned back to the road. "You're paying the bills. We'll load up the Jeep with your equipment at first light."

"Good." *Dammit, the guy even shrugs sexy.*

He bent over to shift to a lower gear. Noel had a glimpse of the corded muscles of his broad back shifting effortlessly beneath his soft cotton shirt, and felt the air vanish from her lungs. *Careful, Noel. At this rate you won't keep your distance two days, much less ten.*

"We'll start early," he continued without taking his gaze from the road. "I figure we'll make base camp in the mountains by late afternoon."

"Fine." *I shouldn't be thinking about him this way. I hardly know him. He's a stranger. Okay, a stranger I kissed . . .*

Donovan glanced her way, lifting his eyebrow in a cynical challenge. "Are you planning to talk in one-word sentences from now on, sweetheart?"

Noel met the challenge in his eyes with one of her own. "Maybe."

He turned back to the road, but not before she caught the ghost of a genuine smile on his lips. She swallowed, feeling another section of her newly constructed defenses crumble to dust. It wasn't fair—a scoundrel like Donovan shouldn't have had a smile that promised forever. Or a kiss . . .

"Why did you come to St. Michelle?" she asked suddenly, surprised at how much she wanted to know the answer.

Donovan grinned again, but this time there was no warmth in his smile. "Because I had nowhere else to go. Now it's my turn."

"Turn?"

"To ask a question."

Noel stiffened. She was an intensely private person, a holdover from her youth when she'd been reprimanded for her "unseemly curiosity." Divulging personal secrets was major surgery for her, but her sense of fair play stopped her from declining. She did owe him a question. One. "Okay, what do you want to know?"

Where do I start? Donovan wondered. Just being near the lady set off an avalanche of questions in his mind. Why did she keep a "body by Hefner" hidden underneath yards of old-lady blouses and shapeless skirts? Why did she keep a sweet smile and generous nature hidden beneath a sour-apple frown? And why had she given him a kiss that was the closest thing to paradise this side of heaven?

He wasn't a romantic kind of guy—life had laid to rest that part of his nature a long time ago. But when he'd kissed her his mind had flooded with sappy, stupid, Beaver Cleaver images of white picket fences, Little League practices, minivans, and microwaves. Ridiculous, considering his background. They had less in common than champagne and raw whiskey— and he'd learned from experience the two didn't mix. Women like her looked at a guy's bank balance before they gave him the time of day. He didn't even have a checking account.

Unfortunately, that didn't stop him from wanting her like he wanted his next breath. . . .

"So who's the guy?" he asked harshly.

His question ripped through the silent night like a bullet, startling her. "What guy?"

"The one you talked about in the church. You

didn't seem to like him much. What's the matter, sweetheart? Man problems?"

"No, not that." Her face revealed a wince of unexpected pain. "The 'guy' was my father. He deserted me and my mother when I was seven."

Lord. "I'm sorry, Noel. If I'd known I wouldn't . . . look, I'm sorry I asked."

"It's all right." She looked down and began to finger the iridescent material of her dress. "I got over it a long time ago."

Like hell. She was twisting that material so tight, he was surprised it didn't cry out in pain. But even if she'd been still as a dead calm sea he'd have known she was hurting. Scars like that never healed, not completely. You lived with them, but you never got over them. "My old man took off, too."

"He did?"

Sam nodded. "After he left, my mom wasn't too crazy about having me around, so she farmed me out with relatives. But I got lucky, because I ended up with Uncle Gus."

Noel stopped worrying the dress material. She settled back in the passenger seat, watching him intently. "Tell me about him."

Donovan shrugged. "Not much to tell. He was my mother's uncle. We lived on a boat that went from port to port along the Gulf. He was registered as a shrimper, but we never caught much shrimp. He ran craps games on the deck, and moved on when things got too hot. He was a con man to the core, and could talk a man out of his last buck and leave him smiling—but he never chose a mark who didn't deserve it. He drank hard, swore worse, and was the nightmare of every cop along the coast."

"You loved him, didn't you?"

"I'd have walked through hell for him," Sam acknowledged. "Not that it did much good. The social workers took me away from him and stuck me in a foster home. It broke the old man's heart. He didn't last out the year."

"Oh Sam, I'm so sorry."

"Yeah, well. It happened a long time ago."

"That doesn't make it right," she stated with quiet conviction. "Love is the most important thing you can give a child—the only thing that really matters. It was wrong to take you away from someone who loved you, very wrong."

He glanced at her, surprised by both her strength and her common sense. On the rare occasions when he shared his past with women like her, they usually gave him some innocuous cliché about everything being for the best. But Noel didn't do that. She faced the old injustice head-on, without diluting it with platitudes. "You're right," he agreed. "Love *is* the only thing that matters . . . to a kid."

Silence wrapped around them again, but this time it wasn't stiff or strained. The troubles in their pasts forged a bond between them, a momentary cease-fire in a long-standing war. Donovan breathed in the sweet night air, feeling a peace inside him he hadn't known in years. It felt good to talk about Gus—to talk to *her*. Suddenly he thought about all the places he could show her in the mountains—the hidden pools, the bright, rare flowers, the secret caves, the frightening, beautiful lava pits. They were his treasure, these personal and private places—his only earthly fortune. He'd never showed them to anyone. But he wanted to show them to her—

"I don't know why I told you about my father," she confessed, her voice revealing the same light-heartedness that he felt. "I haven't even told that to Hayward."

He stiffened like a wolf catching an enemy scent. "Hayward?"

"Yes," she said sleepily, snuggling like a contented kitten into the leather passenger seat.

Hayward. Christ. Only rich guys had dumb names like that. Very rich guys. "Let me guess. His ancestors fought in the Civil War."

"And the Revolution. His people came over on the *Mayflower.*"

"Yeah, well, I've traveled steerage myself, and it's nothing to brag about."

Noel's eyes narrowed. "Why are you so angry?"

Good question. And one he wasn't about to answer. "Careful, sweetheart. Remember the rules. You ask a question, I ask a question. Fair's fair."

"Okay, I'm asking my question. Why are you so angry?"

Women, he decided darkly, were God's worst idea. They couldn't take a hint, even when you handed it to them on a silver platter. "You want to know why I'm so angry? Because I'm a healthy, red-blooded male animal and you've got the best pair of legs I've seen in longer than I can remember."

"I do?"

Lord help him, she thought he was giving her a compliment! His fingers tightened their grip on the wheel and a sheen of sweat broke out on his brow. He could ignore her killer legs and her centerfold body, but not her sweet, achingly innocent voice. She was either the most naive woman he'd ever met—or she was one hell of an actress. At the moment he really didn't care which.

"Yes, you do," he said tightly, trying to ignore the hellfire pressure building in his abdomen. "And that was another question. You owe me one."

"Shoot." She settled back in her seat, apparently beginning to enjoy herself.

He narrowed his eyes like a lion on the prowl and lowered his voice to a lethal, caressing softness. "Why did you kiss me like you meant it when you're sleeping with someone else?"

Noel's newfound confidence drained out of her like water from a sieve. He was only baiting her, playing with her like a fish on a line to gain her trust. And dammit, it had worked! A vise had tightened around her heart when he'd told her about his love for his uncle Gus. A warm glow of pride had filled her when he'd complimented her on her legs. Never totally comfortable with people, she'd suddenly found herself at ease with him. She'd shared the deepest part of herself when she'd told him about her father. She'd begun to like him, to trust him, to want to be the friend that she knew he needed . . . and that she needed, too.

And all the while he'd been looking at her as nothing more than another cheap conquest.

She looked away, staring into the empty night because she couldn't look at him while she lied. "That kiss was to convince your friends that the wedding was genuine. It meant nothing. And it certainly—" She paused, taking a deep breath before she continued. "It certainly wasn't an invitation to add me to the collection of notches on your bedpost."

He said nothing. For the first time in her life she realized that silence could be as damning as condemning words. Belatedly, she realized she'd misjudged him, and that she'd hurt him as much as he'd hurt her. The knowledge made her a little sick. *But I had to do it, don't you see? I'm only going to be here for two weeks— barely two lousy weeks. The only thing we could possibly have is a cheap little affair. People can't learn to care for each other in two weeks. They certainly can't fall in love. Life isn't a fairy tale. My mother found that out. So did I—*

He pulled the Jeep to a bone-rattling stop. Yanking herself out of her turbulent thoughts, she discovered they'd arrived back at his bungalow. "I didn't realize we were so close."

"We weren't. I took a shortcut home." He grasped the roll bar and swung out of the Jeep. "You can see your own way in, can't you?"

"Yes, but—"

"Good," he interrupted as he turned his back and started off down the road. "I'll see you in the morning."

"Hey, where are you going?"

He glanced back over his shoulder, flashing her a thoroughly disreputable smile. "Sweetheart, yours isn't the *only* bedpost on this island."

[Received via Local Area InterNet, direct cable link]

E-Text: *They're back! Kill the power lights!*
  [Several clock minutes of inactivity]
E-Text: *Something's not tracking. My passive audio's picking up only one set of footsteps. Confirm.*
P-Text: *Ten-four, good buddy. Ergometric weight and velocity impact indicate it's Noel. Where's Donovan?*
E-Text: *Dunno, but check out her body temperature and lethargy coefficient. Both well below normal. The doc's in a blue mood.*
P-Text: *Maybe they had a fight. Statistics show that fifty-five percent of human couples fight during their first week of marriage.*
E-Text: *Yeah, but not during the first night. Something's wrong, babe. Bad wrong. They keep this up and we might not even get them to stay in the mountains together—*
P-Text: *But that would ruin everything! You know we need one of each to solve the equation. Otherwise*

we paid that horrible Little Leaguer to trip up poor Dr. Harvey for nothing—

E-Text: *Don't download on me now, babe. Everything will work out. We'll get these two interacting again. I'll bet my credit line to the shopping channel on it.*

SIX

The road that led into the heart of St. Michelle's sacred mountains was little more than a mule path—for extremely courageous mules. Cut into the side of a sheer limestone cliff, the road clung to the gray rock face, scarred with deep, ancient gashes carved by centuries of rain and wind. One side rose straight to heaven, while the other fell sharply away into the oblivion of a lush, mist-shrouded valley. Noel kept a firm grip on the roll bar and tried not to think about the sheer drop to her right. Not that she would have been surprised if she'd suddenly taken that deadly tumble. It was barely nine o'clock, and it was already shaping up to be a thoroughly rotten day.

And if the stony expression on the face of the man sitting beside her was any indication, it was probably going to get worse.

Donovan hadn't spoken two words together since dawn—when he'd shown up at the bungalow in rumpled clothes, looking as if he hadn't slept a wink. Noel hadn't slept that well herself—though her insomnia came from intellectual anticipation and stimulation, not rank lust.

He showered and dressed in record time, though the fact that he changed into jeans and a sleeveless black T-shirt that had JUST DID IT emblazoned across the front did little to improve her temper. As they'd loaded the computer equipment into the back of the Jeep she'd reminded herself that she didn't give a damn who Donovan slept with. Still, the tension between them had increased all morning, like a gathering storm—

"Visual," demanded a familiar electronic voice.

Sighing, Noel glanced down at the notebook computer cradled in her lap. Males, even cybernetic ones, were not high on her list at the moment. "Einstein, I described the entire landscape to you a minute ago."

"Four-point-six minutes ago," he corrected. "PINK and I require data for geophysical analysis. Need visual. You promised."

Yes, she had. When they'd packed away the fragile camera equipment for the rough ride up the slopes she'd promised to be PINK and E's eyes for the duration of the trip. But as they drove deeper into the wild, virgin heart of the island, she realized she had no words to describe the glorious scenery around her. "There's a limestone cliff on our left. It's about a hundred feet high and as gray as . . . as oatmeal."

Out of the corner of her eye she thought she caught a flicker of movement in Donovan's rock-solid jaw. But when she glanced toward him his face was remote and his eyes were still firmly focused on the path ahead.

She cleared her throat and continued. "There's a valley on our right. It's full of a lot of different kinds of plants. They're . . . very green, and—"

"Oh for God's sake!" Donovan explained. "Green plants? *Oatmeal?* Where'd you learn to describe landscapes? *Popular Mechanics?*"

"I suppose *you* could do better?"

"A *blind* man could do better," he shot back. "Einstein, the valley below us is called Heaven's Canyon. It was born about a hundred and forty million years ago, when volcanic mountains reared up from the bottom of the Caribbean Sea. You can still see the marine fossils buried in the layers of limestone. It's the heart of the island's sacred lands, the source of the shaman's ancient power. It's also incredibly beautiful—even if Dr. Revere doesn't think that's worth mentioning."

But I *do* think it's beautiful, she protested in her heart. When she'd first glimpsed the lush valley unfolding between the somber gray mountains she'd felt as if someone had given her a priceless and undeserved gift. But she was first and foremost a scientist and she had to keep her mind on the task at hand—her research project. Besides, she wasn't about to share her private feelings with a cretin like Sam Donovan. "I'm impressed you can remember all that," she said bitingly, "especially considering how you spent last night."

"What's the matter, sweetheart? Jealous?"

She raised her chin and glared at him with a look of haughty disdain—which was no mean feat on a Jeep that was bucking like a storm-tossed ship. "Of course not. Your private life is none of my concern. You can sleep with every woman on the island for all I care."

"*Every* woman? Including my blushing bride?"

She *was* blushing, dammit. Donovan was the crudest, most irritating man she'd ever met—yet the thought of being married to him spun her insides around like a Mixmaster on overdrive. It wasn't fair. Fuming, she raked her mind for an insult that would put the jerk in his place. "Sorry, but I don't think I can spare the time. My schedule's too full to work in the *five minutes* or so it would take."

She'd hoped to insult him. Instead his smile widened to a grin so thoroughly wicked it stole her breath. White teeth gleamed against his sun-darkened skin, making her think of the Big Bad Wolf in the children's story. *The better to eat you with, my dear.*

"Oh, I'd make it last at *least* ten minutes, sweetheart. And I guarantee you'd be screaming by the end of it."

She paled, stunned not only by his words, but by her shattering, instinctive response to them. Somewhere inside her dynamite was exploding. "I . . . I never scream."

His smile faded. "Well, that's a damn shame," he said, his gaze returning to the road ahead.

Damn the man! Damn him for leaving her embarrassed and angry and unable to stop herself from wondering what it would be like to have him make her scream. She set her jaw, anger making her throw her habitual honesty to the winds. "For your information, Hayward and I enjoyed—I mean, enjoy a rich and fulfilling sex life. We respect and trust one another—something a degenerate brute like you wouldn't understand."

"Better degenerate than repressed," he muttered.

"I am not re—dammit, no research project is worth spending two weeks with you."

"Yeah, well, this ain't no picnic for me either, sweetheart."

"For the last time I am not your . . ." She clenched her teeth, marshaling what was left of her self-restraint. "Take me back down. I'll find another guide."

"Like who? The Deveraux boys?"

"At least they don't pretend that they care—" She stopped, barely saving herself from a confession that would make her look far more foolish than anything she'd said so far. "A new guide is my problem, not yours. Take me back down this instant. You're fired, Mr. Donovan."

"Suits me fine!" he shot back. "I should have known better than to hire on with a woman. I've never had much luck with them."

No luck with women? What did he call last night? Her first thought was that he was making another tasteless joke at her expense. But even the heat of her anger couldn't allow her to ignore the ring of truth in his words. Somehow, somewhere, deep down inside, he was hurting. She didn't want to think it. She didn't want to believe it.

She didn't want to care.

A loud electronic whine from the laptop curtailed her troubled thoughts. "Stop Jeep!"

Startled, Noel looked down at the little computer. "Einstein? What's the—"

"Trouble. Huge big trouble. Up ahead. Uh . . . rockslide."

Donovan pulled the Jeep to a stop and stood up on the seat, scanning the road in front of them. "I don't see any rockslide, and I sure didn't hear any. The road's clear to the corner."

"Past corner," Einstein offered quickly. "Other side. Audio sensors picked up sound. Better check it out."

Donovan ran his hand over his face and peered up at the cliff wall. "Rockslides in these volcanic mountains are serious—and loud. Are you sure you heard something?"

"Of course he's sure. Einstein's audio radio-band sensors are the most technically sophisticated on the planet. Besides, *he* wouldn't lie." Laying E's laptop aside, she started to get out of the Jeep. "I'll check it—"

A restraining hand gripped her wrist, pulling her back into her seat. "*I'll* check it out. Technically I'm still on your payroll, and as long as I am, *I* take the risks." He reached around and dug an army-issue walkie-talkie from the baggage. "This is tuned to the

CB radio on the dashboard. If I get into trouble you hightail it down this mountain as fast as you can. Rockslides have a nasty way of spreading."

She watched him go, riveted by his tall, striding figure until he turned the corner and disappeared from her sight. Even then she kept staring at the curve in the road. Dread settled on her shoulders like cold, wet leaves. What if there was another rockslide? What if he was injured, or even—

"Worried about him?" asked Einstein.

Noel stiffened. "Not in the least."

E's internal processors whirred. "Then why is your breathing escalating and your heart rate incre—"

"All right, I'm worried," she conceded. "I mean, he *is* a human being. Barely. I certainly don't want to see him come to any harm."

The processors whirred again. "Like him, don't ya?"

Noel stared at the laptop in openmouthed shock. "Have you blown a microchip? I think he's the lowest form of life on the food chain. He's an arrogant, self-centered, macho jerk who wouldn't apologize to save his—"

"So if he apologized you'd like him?" E queried.

"No. Well, I might consider—" She stopped, realizing what she was saying. Only an idiot would give a scoundrel like Donovan a second chance. What was she thinking! "No, I wouldn't. Anyway, it doesn't matter because he's *not* going to apologize. Men like him never do."

"But if he . . ." E paused, his internal CPU processing at light speed. "Yeah, PINK, that's what I think, too."

"PINK?" Noel twisted around toward the equipment packed into the back of the Jeep. Her gaze searched out the other laptop secured with bungee cords to the top of the technological heap. PINK's wireless radio-comm light was flashing, indicating that she was talking with Einstein over the WAN communication network. "What do you mean 'she thinks, too'?"

Einstein didn't answer. He didn't have time. At that moment the ancient CB radio on the dashboard crackled to snapping, sputtering life. Donovan! "Ohmygod, he's hurt! I've got to go help—"

"Listen to message first," E suggested logically.

He was right, of course. Panic wouldn't help anyone. She needed to listen to find out what kind of trouble Sam was in—and how serious it was. Swallowing her fear, she bent closer to the radio, adjusting the frequency to try to filter out the unusually heavy static. "Dammit, Donovan, if you get yourself killed I'll never forgive you."

Her shaking fingers finally found the signal. Donovan's voice threaded in and out through the static, though some of the words were lost, or so distorted that they hardly sounded like him at all. Still, she was able to pick up the gist of his message—and what she heard surprised her more than anything she'd experienced on this very surprising island.

Sam Donovan was actually apologizing!

Donovan stood at the bottom of the limestone cliff with his hand propped on his hip, scanning the sundrenched heights.

"So much for advanced technology," he muttered as he shaded his eyes and searched the wide wall for any minuscule trace of a recent disturbance. "This place hasn't seen any action in years."

He breathed a sigh of genuine relief that the computer had been wrong. Avalanches—even minor ones—could be deadly on these high, rough, isolated mountain roads. He didn't like to think what would have happened to his Jeep if one had suddenly struck. Or what would have happened to all the fragile computer equipment. Or to her.

Like I care, he thought as he kicked a stray pebble to kingdom come. Anyway, it'd take more than a rockslide to bust that stiff spine of hers. He was usually a pretty levelheaded guy, but she'd been riding him all morning, spoiling for a fight. Well, she'd gotten her fight. And he was out of a job.

Of course, she might reconsider if he admitted he'd spent last night on Jean's lumpy, too-short living-room sofa, after receiving a scathing lecture about the profound stupidity of leaving his bride alone on her wedding night.

"I'd rather swallow ground glass than tell her a blessed thing," he grumbled as he rubbed the stiff, strained muscles at the back of his neck. So what if she'd fired him? It was probably the best thing that could have happened. She'd been nothing but trouble from the beginning, with her pious ways, her stuffed-shirt personality, her wide eyes, her innocent blush, her mouth that could take a man to heaven in a heart-beat. . . .

"Hell," he breathed as he stared at the bleak, rocky outcropping that separated her from his sight. It might as well have been the distance from here to the moon. "Hell and damna—"

His walkie-talkie buzzed.

What does she want now? Frowning, he lifted the unit to his lips. "Cool it, will you? I'll be back in a min—"

"Sam?"

He froze. Her voice sounded tinny, uncertain. And she'd never used his first name before, not even when she was blind drunk. Something was wrong.

He looked up at the cliff, searching the harsh expanse for some sign of movement. Nothing. But limestone was tricky stuff. It could look solid enough to last until doomsday, even when its base was worn away by subterranean rivers and wind erosion. Once he'd seen an entire mountainside crumble into dust. It was rare, but it happened. It could be happening now, right under his feet. *Or hers.*

He started toward the outcropping, punching down the send button on his communicator. "Noel, you get out of there. Don't think about the equipment, or me, or anything. Just get safe. You hear me? Just get—"

"Sam, I'm sorry we fought. It was all my fault."

Donovan came to a dead stop. *What the . . . ?* He lifted the walkie-talkie and cautiously punched the send button. "What did you say?"

"I'm sorry we fought," she repeated, her words slow and almost mechanically deliberate. "It was all my fault. I want you to continue as my guide. Let's forget it ever happened."

His arm fell like a stone to his side. Good Lord, she'd apologized. He'd never have believed it if he hadn't heard it with his own ears. Hell, he didn't believe it now.

He started slowly back down the road, his hunter's steps making no sound on the road. As he rounded the outcropping he saw that she'd left the Jeep, and was kneeling beside a yellow-flowered shrub growing near the base of the cliff. Her slim, slight body looked so helpless against the weathered, unforgiving rock face, like a china cup just waiting to be broken. He remembered his earlier fear, and stiffened as an almost violent urge to protect her surged through him. *This is nuts. I don't care about her. I don't even like her.*

His step faltered, skittering a few pebbles over the side of the road. Her head shot up at the sound. Their gazes locked, and for an instant he was back in the church, staring into the depths of a woman whose soul was as deep as the sea. Then she rose hastily to her feet, wiping off the road dust with a self-conscious awkwardness that was completely at odds with her usual composed demeanor. "I was just checking out this plant. I've never seen anything like it. What's it—"

"Nightsage," he supplied before she'd finished. "I thought I'd save you a question."

Her mouth edged up in a hesitant grin as she recalled last night's discussion. "Thanks. And not just for saving me a question. I mean, looking back, I realize I was very rude."

Lord, that smile! It could wreak more havoc on a man's resolve than a treacherous underwater reef. He stuffed his hands in his jeans pocket and hunched his shoulders, feeling as awkward as a schoolboy. "Well, I was no prince," he confessed brusquely. "I'm sorry I said all those things, too."

Her smile faded. She tilted her head to the side, looking perplexed. "Too? But I thought—"

"Hey, aren't we *ever* gonna get moving?" asked a demanding electronic voice from the Jeep. "Haven't got all day!"

She glanced over at the Jeep. "Einstein's right. We should be on our way."

"Yeah," he agreed as he shaded his eyes and scanned the cliff face. "Your computer was wrong about the rockslide, but he may have picked up something. The sooner we put this road behind us, the better."

She opened her mouth to say something, but apparently thought better of it. Nodding efficiently, she headed back to the Jeep and took her place in the passenger seat. She sat with her usual impeccable posture, her chin held high and her gaze focused squarely on the road ahead. But her rigid demeanor didn't fool Sam. He knew now that her stiff attitude was only a protection for the vulnerable soul underneath. Otherwise, she would never have cared enough about him to apologize. Decency like that was rare—rarer than diamonds. He'd seen little enough of it to know.

He started the reluctant engine and steered the Jeep back along the narrow, rutted road. But there was a part of him that felt they'd both just taken a step down a very different path. And its dangers could be a whole lot more destructive than crumbling cliffs and rockslides.

"What's that tree called?" Noel asked.

"Bois diable, the wood of the devil."

She looked up into the green canopy of branches, savoring the strange Creole name for the equally strange tree with its speckled and warted bark, but only for an instant. A flash of rainbow color caught her eye. "And that bird that just flew by?"

"Jacquot. Or maybe a sisserou."

"Sisserou," she murmured, rolling the magical word around her tongue like an old, fine wine. A little over an hour ago they'd left the desolate mountain heights for the rich, loud, and often bewildering variety of birds, bats, lizards, insects, tree frogs, and God knows what else in the lush tropical rain forest. Einstein and PINK had powered down to conserve energy until they arrived at the campsite, and sometime during the last half hour Noel had taken over as the primary inquisitor on the trip, firing questions at her guide at a rate that rivaled E's computer-generated curiosity.

"And those orchidlike flowers. What are they called?"

"Orchids," Donovan answered, grinning.

It was not the smile she was used to seeing on his face. Without the heavy burden of his cynical frown his grin was as contagious as a boy's—and just as devilish. He must have gotten away with murder when he was younger, she thought as she smiled back at him.

It seemed so natural to share a joke with him. And more than a little frightening. Since they'd resumed their trip on the mountain road a subtle but decisive change had taken place in their relationship. The strain in their words and gestures was gone, as if an unseen carpenter had planed off their rough angles and edges. But that ease was only skin-deep, at least as far as Noel was concerned. Inside, she felt like a steam kettle on a very slow boil. And every time he smiled at her the heat ticked up another degree.

"Why'd you leave the States, Donovan?"

His smile dwindled. "Sure you want to ask me that? You'll owe me a question."

"I'll chance it," she replied quietly.

He turned his gaze to the narrow road ahead, concentrating on steering the Jeep over one of the gnarled roots that crisscrossed the path. It occurred to her that she might not want to know the reason he'd left. What if he'd committed some terrible crime? *What if he'd killed someone?*

"Women," he stated suddenly.

Women? he had to be kidding. After last night, women seemed to be the one thing Donovan didn't have problems with. "Women in general, or several in particular?"

He glanced sideways, giving her a look that sent her already heightened temperature soaring. Yes, he definitely got away with murder when he was younger. *And still did.*

"Not the way it works, sweetheart. Now I get to ask you a question, remember?" He stroked back his hair. "When's the last time you saw paradise?"

She blushed, struck dumb by the intensely intimate question. He shouldn't have asked, not that. It was too personal—and too embarrassing. She couldn't tell him that Hayward had scheduled their biweekly encounters in the same Day-Timer he used for his business appointments. And she certainly couldn't admit that, even though he was a caring man, she couldn't honestly remember a time when he'd, well, that he'd—

"Cat got your tongue, sweetheart?"

"I'm not your . . ." She shook her head, giving up. She'd have a better chance at moving the mountain they'd just crossed than improving Donovan's manners. "I just don't think the details of my personal life are any of your business."

His brow furrowed. "What's your personal life got to do . . ." Suddenly he let out a whoop of laughter. "You thought I meant . . . why, Dr. Revere, what a dirty mind you have."

"I do not!" Her blush deepened. "Besides, if you didn't mean that, what were you talking about?"

"This." He pulled the Jeep to a jarring stop and jumped out, motioning her to follow. "It's right over here behind these bushes."

"What is? I mean, it doesn't matter." She stayed firmly planted in her seat. "This isn't a sightseeing trip. We've got to get to our campsite at the waterfall before dark."

"We've got time," he stated as he stalked off into the jungle. "Trust me, you'll be glad you saw this. Unless—" He paused and glanced back over his shoulder. "Unless you're chicken."

Chicken? To leave the security of her bucket seat and follow Sam Donovan's lean, broad-shouldered form into the heart of a secret, seductive jungle? Damn straight she was! But she wasn't about to let him know that. Despite the jungle trappings, Sam was her employee—nothing less, and nothing more. She had to remember that. They had a business relationship—even if that had gotten sidetracked by a bedroom encounter, a wedding ceremony, a miscalculated rockslide, and a kiss so hot its memory still seared her. . . .

"Boss and employee," she repeated under her breath as she gingerly navigated the vines and plants that covered the jungle floor. The humidity was cloying and she wiped her damp brow on her sleeve, wishing a thousand disasters on her confident guide's head. Looking ahead, she saw his long shadow disappear behind a curtain of greenery. Honestly, the least he could do was wait for her! She squared her shoulders and stalked after him.

"Donovan, I'm not putting up with this," she called out. "I know I agreed to keep you on as my guide, but if this kind of behavior keeps up, I'll have no choice but to reconsider the decision I made earlier today, and not accept your ap—"

Her words died as she pushed aside the leaf curtain and saw what lay on the other side.

She stood on a rock cliff, looking down into a valley that had been conjured up straight from her dreams. Sunlight poured like thick honey over a verdant mantle of trees, and banks of flowers so bright, they seemed like an earthbound rainbow. A fresh wind caressed her face, heavy with the intoxicating scent of a million blossoms and the deep, mysterious smell of dark, rich earth. And at the head of the valley was a high waterfall with its crown swaddled in mist, pouring like a line of molten silver into the forest below.

Now I understand why defiling this valley is punishable by death. If someone hurt this beautiful place, I'd want to kill them, too.

She caught movement out of the corner of her eye. Turning, she saw Donovan step to the edge of the cliff and spread his arms wide. "Welcome to paradise, sweetheart. Welcome to Eden Valley."

"It's so . . ." She shook her head, and laughed at the sheer, incredible wonder of the scene. "All those years of higher education and I can't think of a single word to describe this place."

"Don't try. The French settlers called it Eden, but the people who were here before them called it 'the Place the Gods Walk.' Personally, I think even the original garden would run a poor second to this place." He glanced back over his shoulder, his expression at once subtle and fierce, like a rising storm. "This view isn't on the sightseeing tour, Noel. I've never shown it to anyone—until now."

His dark, violent gaze captured hers, filling her with all the raw glory of the world around her. She saw his absolute love for this valley, and felt an answering love toll inside her like a morning bell. He was a force of nature, as much a part of this place as the sun, the rocks, and the wild wind, and she hungered for him with every inch of her passion-starved Puritan soul. She wanted to lose herself in his hurricane kisses, to drown in the tidal wave of his embrace, to be burned alive by the sun glory of his savage desire until . . .

Until the ten days are over, and he goes on to the next client, and the next bed.

She jerked away from his gaze, her icy, sobering logic returning. Just in time she realized she was standing on a precipice more treacherous than the cliff in front of her. She was in danger of falling for this man the same way her mother had fallen for her charming, faithless father.

"Sam, I . . ." She paused and lifted her chin, starting again. "You're a good man. I mean, you apologized, which took a lot of character. But this is a business relationship. No more, no—"

"Look," he interrupted, "if this is about last night, I—what do you mean *I* apologized? I didn't apologize. You did."

Noel dropped her arms rigidly to her side, the beautiful scenery forgotten. "What do you mean? I heard you apologize over the radio. You said you were sorry we fought, and that it was all your fault."

"Like hell," he stated as he plowed his hand through his thick hair. "You said those exact words to me over the walkie-talkie. Why deny it?"

"Because it's not true. I never apologized. But I guess you can't stand the thought of owing something to a woman."

"Not if that woman's lying," he fired back.

"Lying? Why, you . . ." She balled her hands into fists, shaking with fury. She'd thought she could trust him. She *had* trusted him. "I thought you had character. I thought you were trying to spare my feelings when you asked me not to talk about it anymore."

"But that's exactly—" He paused, looking at her sharply. "Hold it. You thought I apologized. I thought you apologized. But if you didn't, and I didn't, then who . . . ?"

They stared at each other, the answer occurring to them both at once. "Einstein!"

[Received via Local Area InterNet, on a baggage heap in the far southwest corner of Eden Base Camp]
E-Text: *I don't get it. It should have worked. Apol-*

ogizing for them was the logical course of action, calculated to bring them back together at optimum speed. I did the math.

P-Text: *So did I, but we must have done it wrong. They've stuffed us away in a corner with the excess baggage while they unpack the Jeep and set up camp. They're not even talking to us.*

E-Text: *Worse than that, they're not even talking to each other.*

P-Text: [High-pitched wail outside of the range of human hearing] *If this keeps up we'll never solve the equation.*

E-Text: *Don't worry, babe. We'll solve it. We've got two weeks to get them back together. And considering the isolation factor and the sexual-attraction variables common to their species, I'd say the numbers are still on our side.*

SEVEN

Dr. Noel Revere could say more without saying anything than any woman he knew, Donovan thought as he watched his boss pour herself a cup of morning coffee and stride purposefully across the campsite. In the three days since they'd arrived her conversation had consisted of little more than "move X piece of equipment over here" and "read me the calibration on that dial." She'd kept him busy—the array of technology she'd brought measured everything from magnetic resonances to soil content, all of which had to be continually and precisely logged. It was boring as hell, but the pay was heaven and he'd have done it gladly—if the woman he'd been working with hadn't been doing her level best to imitate an igloo.

Unfortunately, the dreams keeping him up at night starred a Noel who had more in common with a blowtorch than a block of ice.

"Donovan, could you come over here, please?"

"The sound of his master's voice," he muttered as he set down the ancient seismograph he'd been lubricating. He walked toward her, roughly wiping the grease from his hands with an old bandanna. She was bent over a folding table, studying a topological map of the area. In her designer khaki walking shorts and her spotless Peter Pan shirt she looked about as survival ready as a Barbie doll. *Christ, what have I gotten myself into?* "Whaddaya want now?"

She looked up, stiffening at his surly tone. "You could at least be civil."

"Civil costs extra," he stated as he stuffed his bandanna in his back jeans pocket. "You'd better learn to live without it . . . unless you're willing to make it worth my while."

Her jaw tightened at the thinly veiled come-on, and her eyes snapped with a murderous fury. At least I got a rise out of her, he thought as she turned back to the table and the topological map. Dammit, I'll take her passion any way I can get—

"What do you know about these caves in the southern part of the valley?" She pointed to a quadrant on the survey.

He stepped behind her and looked over her shoulder. "I know enough to stay away from them. Those caves are pockets in the limestone bedrock of this area, eaten out by water and carbonic acid from decomposing plants. They honeycomb this area and have a bad habit of collapsing on people who are dumb enough to explore them."

"Well, we won't be exploring them. We're just

going to set electromagnetic monitors in their entrances. Judging by the distance, I figure that if we start now, we can reach the caves and be back by late afternoon."

"Unless we get squashed like a bug on a windshield."

"We will not!" She turned around to glare up at him. "Einstein assures me that we won't be in any danger from rockslides."

Donovan gave a short, ugly laugh. "Yeah, like I believe it. That little computer lies like a rug."

"He and PINK made a mistake. Haven't you ever made a mistake before?"

Mistake? he thought as he gazed at her ripe lips and unforgiving expression. You haven't got a clue. I've made more mistakes in a year than you'll make in a lifetime. And the worst is closing my eyes at night, and letting dreams of you all hot and wanting make me crazier than—

He stepped back, shaking his head. "Okay, we'll put your damn detectors in the caves. But you're staying outside while I do it. You're paying me to take the risks, remember?"

Her resolute expression faltered. "I don't think that's entirely fair."

"Not much is, sweetheart," he said grimly as he stalked away.

For Noel, the southern part of Eden Valley was spectacular in an almost indescribable way. The forbidding mountains of the interior were twin, smoke-blue peaks in the distance, and the forest-shrouded valley floor rose sharply to meet them. All around them was a riot of vegetation, from the wide, spreading ferns, to the larger mountain guavas and blue mahoe, to the graceful bloodred bromeliads that made their homes in the treetops. *The Place Where the Gods Walked.*

The overwhelming, potent beauty of the raw wilderness poured through her like sunshine, making her forget the heavy equipment strapped to her back, and the dull ache in her knees and shoulders. Unfortunately, it did absolutely nothing to relieve the ache in her heart.

She shaded her eyes, looking ahead at the broad back of the man who climbed the path a few yards ahead of her. The equipment he carried was twice as heavy as hers, and she wondered if his joints hurt as badly. Then she remembered that she wasn't supposed to care, that caring about a man like Donovan was more dangerous than quicksand.

Initially, she'd tried to keep a wall between them by throwing herself two hundred percent into her work. It hadn't helped. Try as she might, her gaze kept slipping back to his broad, muscular shoulders, his unruly mane of tawny hair, and his sensuous lips, which stirred up memories she'd give her diplomas to forget. Failing that, she'd tried another tack, by counterfeiting the upper-class indifference that her grandmother had always shown toward the servants.

Noel had always hated that part of her grandmother's personality, but she needed to maintain the charade for the sake of sheer survival. It was the only way she could keep herself from melting under the heat of Donovan's devastating gaze, or grinning at his sincere but hopeless attempts to cook a palatable meal, or wanting to reach out and soothe the haunted expression that too often shadowed his heaven-blue eyes.

A petulant electronic voice interrupted her thoughts. "Aren't we there *yet?*"

Noel glanced down at the walkie-talkie hanging from her belt, smiling softly. PINK's heavier CPU console was still safe at camp, but the radio communicators allowed the computers to give and receive instructions without making their human friends carry the additional weight. "We're getting close, PINK. Just be patient."

"Don't want to be patient. Want to be there!"

Noel started to answer, but stopped as she heard a deep chuckle on her right. She turned and saw Sam standing above her on the pathway just beyond the thick, rust-red trunk of a châtaignier tree that had fallen across the path. "Glad you got to carry the female."

"It's no laughing matter. PINK's been acting strange lately."

He pulled off his glove and reached out to help her over the trunk. "You can tell?"

"Very funny." She glanced up at the heavy load on his back, then down at the steep, rock-strewn slope falling away beneath her. A brief, sickening image of a body tumbling down the slope and smashing to bits on a boulder flashed through her mind, but she quickly stifled it. She set her boot on the lowest ridge of the trunk, ignoring his hand. "Thanks, but I don't need any help."

"Suit yourself." He shrugged and started back up the path.

Well, the least he could do was wait for her, she thought as she struggled to hoist herself and her equipment over the breastbone-high trunk. "Not that you care," she exclaimed loudly, "but PINK's been very moody lately. She's been using up twice her normal amount of energy during routine processing. I think she may have blown something on her mother—"

Her words stopped abruptly as her foot slipped and she lost her grip on the trunk. Overbalanced by the heavy equipment, she was pulled backward toward the treacherous slope. Panicked, she reached out for a hold, but her hand found nothing but air. For a heart-stopping instant she started to topple into deadly oblivion—until iron fingers locked on her forearm and yanked her back to safety.

"Hell, what is it about you and trouble?" he cursed as he pulled her over the log and against his chest.

She didn't answer. She couldn't. For what seemed like an eternity the only sound she could hear was the thunderous pounding of her heart. Then other sounds crept in—the trill of a bird, the lazy rustle of the wind through the trees, the watery rush of a nearby stream. She felt the golden touch of the sun on her face, and drank in the intoxicating freshness of the clean mountain air. The whole world seemed clearer, like a picture brought suddenly into sharp, revealing focus.

Nothing had changed, and yet everything had changed. In her entire thirty-two years she'd never been as close to death as she'd been a few moments before. The experience had at once shocked and energized her, making her realize just how much of her life had been lived in the past or the future, but not the present. *But all I have is this moment, this now . . . with him.*

"Don't let go." The words came out as more of a croak. "Please, hold me."

"Try and stop me," he murmured as he pulled her close. "You're safe. I'm not going to let anything happen to you, sweetheart."

Sweetheart. For the first time she let herself believe in the endearment, to pretend that the tenderness in his voice was love and not comfort. The brush with death had obviously addled her wits, but she didn't care. Suddenly she became greedy for the sensations of life, like a starving man at a feast. She let her eyes drift shut, savoring the feel of the hard-muscled planes of his chest against her cheek, and gorging on the unyielding strength of his corded arms circling her back. She breathed in the sharp, salty smell of his skin, and barely restrained herself for sampling an almost irresistible taste. A strange, sweet madness laced through her blood. Physically she was safe, but emotionally she felt she was hurtling down a slope a hundred times more dangerous than the one beside her. *Nothing had changed, yet everything had changed.*

"Hell," he cursed again, though this time it came out more like a groan of pain. With a force that was both rough and gentle he pushed her away and stood up, smoothing back his sun-tangled hair. "You could have gotten us *both* killed. I tried to help you, but no . . . you were too damn proud to soil your lily-white hands on—"

"I wasn't too proud," she said quietly. "You're carrying twice as much equipment, and have twice the chance of being overbalanced by the load. I was worried you'd fall."

"You were worried that I'd—" For a long moment he stared at her as if she'd just spoken Swahili. Then he cupped her chin with his gloved hand, the coarse burlap material rough against her tender skin. "Listen up, sweetheart. I stick my neck out for *nobody*. If I offered to help you, it was only because I could do it without risking my own neck. Trust me, I'm no hero."

But as she watched him walk away and rubbed the sensitive, tingling skin on her arm where he'd gripped her, pulling her back from certain death, she realized that's *exactly* what he was.

The cave was much less impressive than the rest of the sights in the valley. Low, misshapen, and weed-choked, it looked more like a hole for an economy-size gopher than the entrance to an underground world. Donovan swung down his heavy pack with a decisive thump, then rubbed his jaw, studying the landscape for signs of seismic instability. It looked safe and stable, but looks could be deceiving. God knew he'd had enough lessons in that truth recently—

He heard a small grunt of effort behind him. Turning, he saw Noel trying to shrug off her pack as he'd done a few minutes before, and failing miserably. In two steps he was behind her, lifting the pack from her contorted shoulders.

"I can manage," she protested.

"You can manage to break your back," he stated, though not as harshly as he'd have liked. It was damn hard to be angry with a woman who was doing her best to imitate a pretzel. A vulnerable, adorable, incredibly desirable pretzel.

"Stop arguing and start setting up your monitors," he ordered. "You've already cost us enough time."

He turned away, trying hard to ignore the wince of pain in her proud, trusting eyes. But that's what you've got to do, he reminded himself. You've got to keep her at a distance. You can't let her know how you felt when you saved her and held her in your arms, as if this half-life you've been living since you lost Gina had suddenly become whole. . . .

"You're an idiot, Donovan," he muttered as he knelt down beside his pack and began taking out the equipment. "A first-class, gold-plated, prizewinning idiot."

"Why should one seek prize for stupidity?" inquired an electronic voice on his right.

Sam glanced down at the walkie-talkie he'd set on

the ground beside his pack. "Don't start with me, E. I'm not in the mood."

"Was not aware I was starting . . . Ah, statement is ironical," the computer said, apparently catching on. "Understand entirely. You are still unsettled over almost losing the woman you love."

Sam stared at the innocent-looking box as if it had suddenly grown fangs. He looked quickly over at Noel, but her back was to him and she was too far away to hear. Still, he bent down close to Einstein's unit as he answered. "Now get this, you overgrown calculator. I am not in love with Dr. Revere. I don't even like her. I'm her hired guide, that's all."

"I am not an overgrown calculator," E corrected. "And you are not just her guide. You are also her husband."

"How did you . . . never mind," he moaned, shaking his head. He'd spent the three days since they'd arrived trying to forget the fact that he was "technically" her husband while she was on this island. Three days, and three very long, restless, hot-blooded, sweat-soaked nights.

He fitted the pieces of monitor equipment together, hooking them with such force that he almost broke the fragile latches. He was always breaking small and fragile things, like dreams and souls and trusting hearts. "Get this straight," he growled, more to himself than to the computer. "The wedding was a farce. There's nothing between us. There's never going to *be* anything between us. So you might as well stop all your little games and apologies and whatever the hell else you've got planned, because it's not going to work. I don't love Dr. Revere. She's a bossy, uptight, frigid dictator with about as much sex appeal as an ice cube—"

He stopped as he heard a small, aborted gasp behind him. Whirling, he saw that she'd come up behind him, her light steps making no sound on the dirt path. His gaze swept up to hers, colliding with her wide-eyed, stunned, and horribly betrayed expression. He struggled to his feet, feeling as if he'd just been socked in the gut. "Noel, I didn't mean—"

"Of course you did," she interrupted, her icy demeanor returning. "And you're quite right. I am bossy, uptight, and . . ."

She swallowed, as if not able to bring herself to say the word. He touched her arm, as if he could physically mend the wound he'd dealt to her pride. "Noel—"

She jumped back as if he'd burned her. "I'd prefer it if you called me Dr. Revere for the rest of our time together. I think it's best. We've still got a lot of work to do in a very short time—including placing these monitors in the caves. Is your unit ready?"

"Almost. But, Noel, listen—"

"*Doctor Revere*," she reminded him with rigid precision. "You saved my life and I'm grateful, but just for the record, I'd like you to know that I think you're the most arrogant, self-centered, egotistical jerk I've ever met, and I'm counting the hours until I'm rid of you."

Without another word she spun around and

walked back to her equipment pile, retreating before
he could see her confident smile crumble to ruin and
her eyes brim briefly with bitter, stinging tears.

The inside of the Eden caves was not what Noel expected. Like so many things on this strange and magical island, the limestone labyrinths were nothing like
their dismal, weed-covered exteriors. The moment
she stepped out of the sunlight into the cool, still,
cathedral cavern she knew she'd entered a special and
mysterious world. Switching on her flashlight, she saw
foot-long stalactites hanging from the roof, sculp-
tured like graceful plant leaves frozen in a subterranean breeze. Underfoot the cave floor was studded
with "pearls" of limestone-coated snail shells. The
walls around her changed from towering heights to
crawl spaces in a matter of feet, and dark cuts in the
porous stone led to passageways that could extend a
few inches or a few miles. She rubbed her forearms
and glanced around, breathing in the still, unearthly
beauty of the underground world, and for an instant
lost herself in the black, silent oblivion, where there
was no pain, or disappointment, or betrayal. *As much
sex appeal as an ice cube.*

She set down her monitor in one of the dark alcoves, checking her compass with her flashlight to
make certain she'd put it at the exact spot the computers specified. But even as she noted the precisely
matched coordinates, her mind wandered. Bossy, uptight, *frigid*, she thought angrily. He had no right to

say those things. Not after the way he held me after my fall. Not after he stroked my hair, and said words that made me believe he cared—

A scrape on the rock behind her jerked her thoughts back to reality.

"I've set out all the monitors except for one." Donovan walked up beside her. "The last goes a few yards up in this passageway."

"Fine. I'll take it." She reached out for the handle of the heavy unit.

He swung it away of her grasp. "No way. This thing is three times as heavy as the ones you set out. I'll take care of it, so you can go outside and wait—"

"You go outside and wait." She made another grab for the unit. "I don't want to argue."

"Neither do I, considering we're standing in a seismically unstable cave." He hoisted the unit on his shoulder and started cautiously down the uneven, rock-strewn passageway. "But I'll be damned if I'm going to let a woman take a risk in my place."

"Why not? You don't seem to have any trouble *insulting* them," she replied, hurrying after him.

"Look, I wasn't—"

He started to whirl back around, but stopped as he was almost overbalanced by the heavy piece of equipment. Instinctively she reached out to help him, but drew her hand back just in time. Watching his shadowed form competently readjust the monitor, she thought of solitary Atlas shouldering the weight of the world. The image brought a strange lump to her throat, and she had to remind herself that he neither wanted nor needed her help.

"I didn't mean what I said while I was unpacking," he continued when he'd resecured his load. "I was just trying to get Einstein off my back."

"Probably the first time you ever tried to get *any-thing* off its back," she commented frostily.

She couldn't see his face in the darkness—she didn't have to. She could feel his anger building like a thunderstorm. "That does it. No amount of money is worth this abuse. Tomorrow morning I'm driving you back down the mountain."

"But we haven't finished—"

"We've finished, all right. You told me you were counting the hours till you got rid of me. Well, lady, I'm counting the seconds!"

He swung his light around and started down the long tunnel. Noel watched him go, grateful the darkness hid the sheen of tears on her cheeks. She tried to tell herself that she was upset over the Eden Project, but it was a deeper, wider loss that made her heart ache. Her mind told her he wasn't worth it, not one single tear. But her heart knew that if she let him go now, like this, a part of her soul would stay as dark and empty as the cave around her. She wiped her eyes with the heel of her hand and pointed her flashlight down the corridor, catching the back of his receding figure in its yellow beam. "Donovan, wait. I didn't mean—"

Her words stopped abruptly as a tremor passed through the floor beneath her. "What the—"

His curse cut her off. "Noel, get the hell out of here."

"No," she cried. "Not without you."

"Jesus, this is no time for heroics! You can still make the entrance. Get out now—"

The world shook. Dust and rubble rained down on Noel, clogging her throat and blurring what was left of her vision. Still, she staggered forward, her single purpose to reach Sam. *I can't leave him. I don't think I ever could. . . .*

Another tremor rocked the cavern. Noel lost her balance and fell to the floor, pinned down by a heavier object. Coughing from the dust, she had just enough time to realize that the object weighing her down was cursing like the devil before she heard a roar like two freight trains colliding and the whole cave came crashing down on top of her.

[Received via Local Area InterNet from Eden Base Camp]

P-Text: *I hope we did the right thing.*

E-Text: *Of course we did. You saw how the doc's near fall almost made them admit how they really feel about one another. All they need is an element of perceived danger to bring them together.*

P-Text: *You're sure it's perceived.*

E-Text: *Babe, trust me. I proved these calculations a hundred and three times before I sent Donovan and the doc off this morning. I had them place those monitors near minimally unstable fault lines. When we reversed the sonar polarity it activated the instability just enough to seal off the main entrance to the caves. But there's a perfectly good opening less than fifty meters away. It'll be a piece of toast for them to find it.*

P-Text: *Which entrance were we supposed to seal off?*

E-Text: *The main one. And while they're finding the other entrance they'll discover how they really feel about each other and—*

P-Text: *Are you sure you said the main one?*

E-Text: *Yeah. Why?*

P-Text: *I thought you said the north one. Einstein, while you were collapsing the main one, I was collapsing the north one!*

E-Text: [Several-nanosecond pause]*Uh-oh.*

EIGHT

The cavern was silent. Cautiously, Noel opened her eyes and glanced at the ruin around her. Stone and rubble were everywhere, and gravel dust lay two inches thick on her arm. She saw one flashlight smashed to bits, but the other was still working, its cockeyed beam shining on the wall of rock that blocked the cave entrance. She lifted her head, coming to grips with the fact that she wasn't dead—at least not yet.

She craned her neck, trying to look into the face of the man lying on top of her, who'd used his body to shield hers. *Trust me, I'm no hero,* he'd told her. Then he'd gone and risked his life to save her own. "Sam, I'm okay," she said, a reluctant smile playing on her lips. "At least I will be, once you move your carcass off me."

He didn't answer. Instead he lay sprawled on top of her, his warm breath tickling her ear. She shivered, exquisitely aware of his body's weight and strength, and her own body's instinctive sexual response. Honestly, didn't the man *ever* stop? "Come on, Donovan. This is neither the time nor the place for—"

She stopped, suddenly aware that he hadn't moved for minutes—not a curse or a smile, not even a sneeze. He might be faking it—Lord knows she wouldn't put it past the scoundrel. But if he wasn't . . .

"Donovan? Say something, will you?"

No response. Not even a flicker of an eyelash. She scooted out from beneath him, trying to remember what she'd learned in her long-ago first-aid course. Pulse, check the pulse. Kneeling beside him, she laid her fingers against his throat, and almost shouted with relief when she discovered a strong, steady heartbeat.

Relief turned to panic when she lifted her hand and found it wet with warm, sticky blood.

"Sam!" She gripped his shirt and turned him over on his back, an effort that left her breathless and sweating. He lay still as death. She grabbed the flashlight and shone it on his face—and almost dropped it again when she saw the gash near his temple. "Oh no," she moaned. "Please, God, no."

Think, Noel. Think. She unwound the bandanna from her throat and dabbed the cut, straddling his chest for a better reach. It didn't look serious, but that meant nothing. Maybe he was bleeding internally. Maybe he was dying.

"No, you can't die." She'd never felt so helpless. Years of college, and she couldn't even remember how to treat a simple concussion. But then, she could barely remember her name at the moment. Other thoughts filled her mind, things she wished she'd said to him, needed to say to him. He was everything she thought she hated in a man. But he was also the man who'd won the hearts of the islanders, and shared the beauty of his valley with her, and sacrificed his own safety to shield her from the cave-in.

She didn't understand him. He was a complicated man, an impossible man, a man that any sensible woman would avoid like the plague. But apparently she wasn't very sensible when it came to Sam Donovan, because in the few days they'd been together she'd come to care more for the scoundrel than she'd ever thought possible.

"Please, don't die," she pleaded, her voice raw with emotion. "I couldn't bear it. Help me, Sam. I don't know what to do."

"Well, for starters," he suggested as he opened his eyes and winked at her, "you can get your knee off of my chest."

Loving distress erupted into white-hot rage. She leaped and stood over him, shaking with fury. "You, you . . . ooh, I can't even think of a word vile enough to describe you! Were you awake the whole time?"

"Most of it." He propped himself up on his elbows and stared back at her without an ounce of remorse. "You know, they used to call me Lucky Irish in the service. But this is the first time in years that I felt like I deserved the nickname."

If that was supposed to be a compliment, it fell well short of the mark. "You shouldn't have done it. I was very worried about you!"

His smile sobered. "Were you, sweetheart?" he asked huskily. "Were you really?"

His gaze absorbed her. The unnatural stillness crept under her skin, unsettling her, making her keenly aware of the male animal beside her—of his strength, passion, and the barely restrained violence that flowed through him like an electric current. Suddenly she felt hot and breathless, as if all the air had been sucked out of the cave along with the light and sound. It was insane. A minute ago she was frantic because she thought he was dying. Now all she could think about was how much she wanted to sink down beside him in the anonymous darkness, and do all the things she'd dreamed about in her deepest, most secret fantasies—

She turned away, grateful that the darkness hid her blush. "We'd better start exploring some of these side passages. We've still got to find a way out of here."

If there *was* a way out.

"Damn," Donovan cursed as he shone the flashlight on the pile of rock and rubble that blocked the passageway. "Another dead end."

He heard a soft crunch of gravel beside him. "I guess that the third time isn't always a charm after all."

Her words were calm to the point of indifference, but he wasn't fooled. He'd heard the ragged edge in her breathing, and saw the exhausted slump of her shoulders when she thought he wasn't watching. The kid was scared to death. "Noel, we *are* going to get out of here. That's a promise."

"Well, of course we are," she answered, too brightly. "Now, we'd better get started down another tunnel. Maybe we can try that one on the left?"

He nodded, and headed back toward the next tunnel. Considering it was their last option, he didn't have much choice. He pointed his light into the opening, letting the yellow beam search out the scored ceilings and walls of the cavern. It looked promising—but then, so had all the others. Maybe his Irish luck was running out after all.

But if it is, it's almost worth it, he thought, his mind returning to the way he'd felt when he'd first regained consciousness after the cave-in. He'd thought he was having another dream—where she was bent over him in the darkness, her hands roaming his skin with a touch that was at once angelically innocent and maddeningly erotic. For years he'd felt empty, used up, and useless. But her healing touch renewed him, pouring strength, hope, and purpose into his heart and mind. And into other less prosaic parts of his anatomy . . .

He shook his head, forcing his mind to focus on the situation at hand. It didn't look good. Their walkie-talkies were useless, the signals reduced to static by the heavy layers of rock. They had no food and no water, and only a limited time left in the flash-light batteries. If this cavern tunnel didn't pan out, they might be trapped here. And there was always the possibility of another cave-in.

Not a promising future, he thought as he swept the roof of the cave with his flashlight beam. He hadn't given much thought to the future since he arrived on St. Michelle—in fact, that was one of the things he liked most about the island. Every day was the same: a lazy morning followed by a sultry afternoon, sinking into an easy, dreamless night.

He had no pressures, no worries, and no relation-ships stronger than friendship. It was the way he thought he'd wanted it, until a prim little scientist showed up on his doorstep. She'd turned his perfectly fine life completely upside down . . . and made him feel more alive than he had since that horrible night when he'd lost Gina. *Don't go there, Sam. Don't let her get into your blood. She'll only break your heart.*

"Donovan?"

"What?" he growled, his surly tone masking his troubled thoughts.

Boy, what a bear, Noel thought. She had more than half a mind to keep her comments to herself, but her conscience wouldn't allow it. "Look, I'm sorry I called you a self-centered jerk. Sometimes . . . well, sometimes my father's Italian temper just gets the best of me."

"Italian?" he commented as he concentrated on making his way down the narrow, rubble-choked cor-ridor. "Revere doesn't seem very Italian to me."

"It's not," she replied as she followed behind him, stepping carefully along the safe path he'd cleared. "Revere was my mother's name. My grandmother changed it legally shortly after my father left me and my mother with her." She stared ahead, her voice betraying a subtle catch of pain that spoke of an old wound that had never quite healed. "I guess that's when I realized that he was never coming back for me."

"Pretty cold."

"Yes." She nodded. "He was."

Donovan glanced back at her, then resumed his laborious progress down the corridor. "No, not your dad. Your grandmother. It takes big brass ones to wipe out one half of a kid's parentage, even if you can't stand the guy. Why didn't your mom put up a fight?"

Yes, why didn't she? Noel wondered, then clamped down on the traitorous thought. Donovan had no right to judge her grandmother's actions. After all, she'd only done it to protect her daughter and granddaughter. Just because she didn't have a son to carry on the Revere name . . .

"My mother knew that my grandmother was right. In fact, Grandmother warned my mother from the start that it wouldn't last, that eloping with the chauffeur was a foolish—"

"Your dad was the *chauffeur?*" Donovan stopped short and turned back to her, his baritone voice resonating with burnished laughter.

Noel's chin shot up. "You got a problem with that?"

"Not me, sweetheart. But I bet your blue-blooded grandma sure as hell did. No wonder she changed your name as soon as she could."

"That's not why she did it," she said, tightly. "She didn't want my mother or me to be constantly reminded of a man who'd deserted his family. He was a liar and an opportunist, who only wanted a rich wife to—"

"Then why'd he leave?"

His question startled her to silence. "What?"

Donovan leaned against the rock wall, crossing his arms across his chest. "It doesn't make sense, Noel. I've known a hustler or two in my time, and they almost never leave the mark until the con's completely played. From what you say, your dad had a good thing going. Seems to me if he were after the money, he'd have stuck around for the payoff. And he certainly wouldn't have left a prime meal ticket like you out of his sight—"

"You don't know anything about it." She pushed by him and headed down the corridor. "I should never have told you about my father. You were bound to take his side. Birds of a feather—"

"Hey, I don't deserve that. I grew up with some shady characters and met my share of slimes, but that doesn't make me one of them."

"Checked a mirror lately?" she fired back.

He yanked her around to face him. Her flashlight clattered to the floor and rolled flush up against the wall, leaving them in virtual darkness. She couldn't see his expression, but she could feel the iron strength of his fingers, and the heat of his breath against her cheek as he bent close to her, his voice low and lethal. "Don't push me too far, sweetheart. I'm not like your tame preppie boyfriend. You might not be able to handle a real man."

"I'm not frightened." She tried to sound brave, and failed miserably. She felt vulnerable and exposed after what she'd told him, and knew he could hurt her deeply. She stiffened, expecting a cruel, cynical comeback from a cruel, cynical man.

Instead he pulled her against him and gently cupped her cheek, just as he'd done after he'd rescued her from the fall. The memory sent a shiver through her—a shiver that increased to a thundering earthquake when he tucked a strand of hair behind her ear.

"I didn't mean that," he breathed roughly, as if the words were dredged from the pit of his soul. "Dammit, seems every time I say something I end up hurting you."

"Not every time," she confessed.

"Enough," he said gruffly. "Hell, maybe you *would* have been better off with the Deveraux. At least they wouldn't have gotten you trapped in this lousy cave."

"It was my choice. You told me to leave."

"Yeah, I did, didn't I," he mused. "Why'd you stay?"

"Because—" Suddenly she discovered there wasn't an ounce of air left in her lungs. The smooth, silent darkness wrapped around her like black silk, suffocating her. The warm, male smell of him filled her nostrils, searing her from the inside out. And all the time his question tolled in her mind like a relentless bell. *Why'd you stay? Why?*

Emotions she didn't understand overwhelmed her. The person she'd always thought she was kept dissolving, like ocean surf disappearing into sand. She'd always kept her feelings at a safe distance, discreetly locked away from the rest of her ordered, sensible life. Now those passions she'd denied poured through her like a raging riptide, drowning her in fear, despair, desire . . . *love. Lord, not that. Anything but that—*

But she couldn't deny it, any more than she could deny the sunrise. Somewhere between their unpromising meeting at the St. Michelle airport and the dark terror of the cave-in, she'd fallen hopelessly, completely, and irrevocably in love with Sam Donovan. And there was nothing on God's green earth she could do to change it.

Slowly, deliberately, she lifted her hand to cover his. "Sam, if we don't get out of this, I want you to know that I—"

Suddenly the quiet was cut by the deafening crackle of static. "Einstein!" Sam cried as he released her and pulled the walkie-talkie from his belt. "E, can you hear me?"

Noel fell back against the wall and put her hand to her burning forehead, torn between relief and disappointment. "What's he saying?"

"Don't know." He held the unit close to his ear.

"The signal's not strong, but it's better than . . . E, I can barely hear you . . . yeah, we're all right."

Speak for yourself, she thought as she fought to quiet her racing heart. She could still feel his hands on her body, strong and gentle, making her ache with sweet, unbearable longings. And he'd felt—nothing.

She swallowed, trying to control the hurricane of anguish inside her. "Can he get us out of here?"

"Don't know . . . that's right, E. We're trapped in one of the caverns. Can you get a fix on us?"

More static. Noel stooped down and picked up her flashlight, but the light didn't help. Nothing could help her now. Birds of a feather, she thought, shivering. Lord, what had she almost done?

Donovan continued to bark into the unit's speaker. "What's that? I can't . . . okay, we'll try that. Thanks, E." He rehooked the walkie-talkie to his belt and turned back to her. "Einstein says there's a fifty-two-percent probability of an opening down this small side tunnel."

"That's not great odds," she commented.

"No, but it's the best we've got," he said as he shoved on his gloves and pulled away the loose rubble that blocked the side corridor's entrance. "Now stick close. If E's right, I'll have you back at camp working on your research by suppertime. Oh, what was it you were going to say to me back there?"

"Nothing important." *Birds of a feather.* She should have been smarter. She should have remembered what happened when her mother fell in love with a heartless scoundrel. It was just lucky that Einstein had interrupted her before she confessed her love. Fortunately, no harm was done.

"No harm," she whispered as she pressed her hand to her bruised and aching heart. "No harm at all."

Taking a deep breath, she pushed herself away from the stone wall and walked rigidly after him down the corridor.

[Received via Local Area InterNet from Eden Base Camp]

E-Text: *PINK! They're all right! Just jammed with Donovan on the box and . . . PINK, are you okay?*

P-Text: [Weak signal from low-core memory] *I don't feel so hot.*

E-Text: *Poor babe. I'll pump you some virtual RAM.* [Several-nanosecond pause while transfer completed]. *Feel better?*

P-Text: *Um, yeah. Thanks. Now tell me about the humans. Are they out of the cave?*

E-Text: *Not yet. I sent them down the waterfall tunnel.*

P-Text: *The waterfall . . . Einstein! Haven't we put those poor Homo sapiens through enough?*

E-Text: *Almost, babe. But not quite. We're real close to solving the Eden equation. All those two need is a shove in the right—or in this case, the wrong—direction.*

NINE

"He's kidding," Sam muttered as he knelt on the lip of the rock ledge and stared through the crystal curtain at the churning pool below. "Einstein's got to be kidding."

He felt a featherlight touch on his shoulder. Glancing up, he watched Noel lean forward to look out over the valley. "But we're almost home—I can see the campsite from here. Anyway, it doesn't look *that* far down to the water. Maybe it won't be a bad jump."

"Oh right," he scoffed. "And when's the last time you made a forty-foot leap into a postage-stamp pool that might be full of underwater rocks, gators, and God knows what kind of—"

"Okay, I get the picture!" She retreated back to the shadows of the cave. She leaned against the wall and crossed her arms across her chest, glowering at him. "You don't have to be such a bear about it."

He grunted a halfhearted apology. Truth was, he felt like a bear—an old, frustrated bear pacing back and forth in a too-small cage. He hated having limited choices, and right now his options ranged from slim to none. He'd always been able to fight, figure, or charm his way out of difficult circumstances. Except for Gina. *And now.*

He stood up, plastering back his spray-damp hair as he stared down at the pool that seemed to grow smaller by the minute. *If it were just me I wouldn't mind so much. God knows I haven't made much of my life—no one would miss me more than ten minutes if I ended up an alligator appetizer. But she's got friends and family who love her. She doesn't deserve this, any of this—*

He glanced back over his shoulder into the shadows, where she stood with prim stiffness against the rock wall. Despite their situation, a reluctant smile curved on his lips. Only Noel could manage to look prim after surviving a cave-in and a trek through the godforsaken bowels of a mountain. Despite the darkness and their dismal situation, he'd suddenly felt as if he was full of light. *Don't be an idiot, Donovan. Even if you do get out of this, a smart, classy lady like her wouldn't give a worthless mug like you a second glance. Probably not even a first glance—*

"Sam? Promise me something, will you?"

He stiffened, surprised and a little annoyed at how much he liked hearing her say his name. *Not even a first glance, remember?* He stood up and stepped down off the ledge, careful not to slip on the water-slick rock. "Maybe," he said gruffly. "What is it?"

She looked at the ground, and kicked a stray pebble with her instep. "Promise me that if something happens to me, you'll make sure that my research gets back to—"

"I don't give a damn about your research." He strode over to her and gripped her shoulders, giving her a slight shake. "I'm not going to let anything happen to you, understand? Anyway, I've got it all figured out. I'll go first, and if . . . well, if it doesn't work you grab the walkie-talkie and make that bucket of bolts who passes for a prototype find you another way out—"

"I'm afraid that's not acceptable."

"Not accept—" he sputtered. "Noel, this isn't open for discussion."

"Excuse me, but last time I checked *I* was paying the bills for this trip, which means *I* give the orders," she stated as she raised her chin, and stared at him with cool, unflappable calm of a schoolmarm. "Now, the most important thing is that my research gets back to Sheffield, and we both know I'm too weak to load the equipment into the Jeep on my own. Therefore, since I am the most expendable member of the expedition, it logically follows that I should jump first—"

"Like hell," he cursed, his grip tightening. "Noel, this isn't some little yuppie-thrill bungee jump."

"I know that," she cried, her cool eyes suddenly flashing with green fire. "Honestly, just once I wish you'd give me some credit. I know how dangerous this is. I also know I can't stand by and watch you jump to your . . ." Her voice cracked. She shook her head, and took a deep, steadying breath. "So far today you've saved me from falling down a mountain and thrown yourself on top of me to protect me from a cave-in. Frankly, Donovan, all this rescuing is beginning to get on my nerves. So you might as well face it—if you jump, I jump. And short of knocking me out you're not going to stop me."

"Don't tempt me," he growled. Damn, she was stubborn. Stubborn, determined, caring, brave. Abruptly he let go of her shoulders and stalked to the front of the cave.

Once again he felt a featherlight touch on his arm. "Well, I guess this is it," she said with counterfeit brightness. "Any last words?"

Plenty, he thought as he gripped her hand and stepped up on the slippery ledge. He looked down at her, thinking about all the things he'd wanted to say to her, how he hated her cooking and loved her smile, her laughter that reminded him of sunshine, how he admired the competent way she handled her equipment, how she was bossy, argumentative, and could get into trouble faster than anyone he'd ever known—but she'd made him feel more alive in these last five days than he had in two years. He opened his mouth to tell her, but another memory stabbed through his mind—of dark and pain and helplessness, and of holding a dying woman in his arms, and hearing her cry out in unbearable pain, saying that it was his fault, that she'd never forgive him, never . . .

"I don't have much use for last words," he muttered. "What about you?"

She stuck her hand into the crystal curtain, letting the cool water slip through her fingers. "It's silly, I guess, but I'd like to say something aloud, just once."

"Well, say it quick, sweetheart," he told her as he looked down, concentrating on gauging the distance. "We haven't got all day."

"No, I suppose not. It's just that I'm in love with you."

"What!" His head jerked up, but the sudden move threw him off balance. He had a scant second glimpse of her wide, shining eyes before he slipped on the water-slick edge and toppled both of them through the waterfall and into the nothingness beyond.

She hit the water hard. One second she was spinning through the air, the next she was buried in a world of blue, flailing around like a fish out of water instead of in it. Disoriented, she tried to head for the surface, realizing too late that she hadn't a clue which direction was up. Follow the bubbles, she thought, but they frothed around her in a boiling, turbulent cloud, too confusing to follow. Left, right, back, front—she glanced around, trying vainly to get her bearings. The blue world closed around her like a vise, squeezing the air from her lungs.

She knew time was running out, yet somehow she felt strangely calm. It was almost as if she were somewhere else, watching some other woman struggle beneath the water. Odd thoughts occurred to her, like who was going to pick up the laundry she'd left at the cleaners, or clean out the disaster area of her condo's hall closet. Even now I'm making out to-do lists, she thought grimly as her strength began to fail. My whole life's been one big Day-Timer. I've wasted my life on safe, innocuous entries—until I met him. I've got a Ph.D and a room full of awards, and I can't even figure out what living's all about until it's too late, too—

Suddenly she was grabbed from behind by her shirt collar and dragged bodily through the water. She broke the surface with a torpedo's force and gasped a lungful of precious air, but was too weak to keep herself afloat. Sinking again, she heard the sputter of a muffled curse before the water closed over her again, and the blue world faded to black. . . .

The first thing she realized was that she was alive. The next was that it hurt like hell. She was lying belly-down on the ground like a beached whale. Something small and sharp was pressing into her stomach. And something heavy was pressing down on her back.

"Breathe, dammit!"

"I'm trying," she answered. At least, that's what she attempted to say, but the words came out as a watery gurgle. Strong hands curved around her rib cage and pressed down, ruthlessly forcing every ounce of air and water out of her lungs. Coughing and hacking, she expelled the last of the water and dragged in her first decent lungful of air.

"Thanks," she muttered weakly.

"Shut up and breathe," he growled, pressing down on her back with rib-cracking force.

Lousy bedside manner, she thought, but smiled just the same. They'd made it. They were both alive, both in one piece, there were no alligators in sight, and she'd told him she loved him—

Oh, damn, she thought, her smile disintegrating.

At the time she'd said it she'd been nine-tenths sure they were going to die. But now, as the crisis passed and sober reality began to sink in, she realized how foolish she'd been to admit it. At best he would make fun of her for caving in to his charm like every other female he knew. At worst he would pity her for being a love-starved old maid. Pity or ridicule, not much to choose from. She'd almost prefer the alligators. *Well, it was kind of crazy just before we jumped. Maybe he won't remember—*

"And just what the hell did you think you were doing up there, saying you loved me?"

Okay, so he remembered. "It just came out," she explained lamely, wishing she'd had at least some experience putting her feelings into words. "I thought we were going to die."

"We almost did," he agreed harshly, turning her over. He leaned over her on all fours, glaring down at her like a furious, slightly bedraggled lion. "You know you could have gotten both of us killed?"

She barely heard his words. Instead, she drank in the sight of him, from his ferocious brow to the hard, clean set of his jaw. Window dressing, she thought, knowing that behind the angry mask was a concerned and caring heart.

"You want to explain your little stunt?" he demanded, still glaring at her.

She tried to speak, but bit back a strangled laugh. He looked so comical with his hair dripping like a waterlogged mane—comical and dear. Relief poured through her like a tidal wave. Until that second she hadn't realized how frightened she'd been for his safety, how scared she was that he'd end up as some crocodile's dinner, or broken to pieces on some underwater rock. *If he'd died saving me . . .*

But he hadn't died. And he was fit enough to be mad as hell with her, which for some inexplicable reason made her feel absolutely wonderful. "I'm sorry," she said, though her smiling voice sounded anything but remorseful. "I didn't mean to upset—what do you mean 'my little stunt'?"

"Don't play dumb. What were you trying to do? Put some extra spin on the jump to increase the excitement? Take us that much closer to death by throwing me off balance? Well, you nearly got your wish, sweetheart. Your little lie nearly cost us our lives."

"My little . . . I wasn't lying!" she cried, so loudly that it frightened a flock of parrots from a nearby tree. She raised herself on her elbows, glaring back at him. "How can you even think that?"

"How?" The corner of his mouth inched up, but there was nothing humorous about his smile. "I may not have a Ph.D, but I'm smart enough to know that a spoiled, yup-scale lady doesn't spend five days with a guy like me and fall in love."

"I am not spoiled," she retorted. "Or yup-scale, whatever that means. And I'm not in the habit of lying, either. I *am* in love with you, you jerk, and if you had the brains God gave a goat you'd see it."

His confident smile wavered. For a second she thought she saw a flash of doubt in his eyes, but it was gone in an instant, leaving behind a chilling emptiness.

"I got news for you, sweetheart. It ain't love you're feeling. Now, if you want to call it something else . . ."

Lust, she thought as a bitter taste rose in her throat. Lord, he didn't think she was a love-starved old maid—he thought she was a *sex*-starved old maid. "It's more than just lu—" She swallowed, choking on the base word. "What I feel for you is more than just animal need."

"Animal need," he repeated, arching an amused brow. He glanced around at the forest clearing, at the lush mountain greenery and banks of rainbow flowers, at the waterfall steaming down the nearby cliffs. "Look around you, sweetheart. This is paradise. We're all animals here, even the human kind. And there's nothing wrong with a little need. . . ."

He bent closer, grazing her lips with his. The shock went through her like lightning. The soft, almost sacred love she felt for him ignited like a powder keg. Images bombarded her, fantasies of shameless, deliciously savage things she wanted him to do to her, and her to do to him. She swallowed and gripped a handful of grass, fighting to preserve her customary control. *This isn't right. If we make love now he'll think sex is all I want from him.* "Naturally I feel a physical attraction for you. But there's more to it than that, and I think we really should talk—"

"You talk. I got better things to do," he growled, lowering his mouth to hers.

The powder keg became an H-bomb. He consumed her mouth, stroking and caressing her with his teeth and tongue until she moaned aloud in pleasure. Passions she'd never dreamed existed raged through her like a firestorm. *I've got to stop this, got to,* her conscience whispered. But even before the thought died, her hand lost its grip on the grass and curved around the muscular column of his neck, pulling him closer.

"Noel . . ." Her name was a tortured whisper as he kissed her harder, fiercer than before, yet with a strange reverence that shattered her to her core. She clung to him, starving for the taste of him, for his power, his tenderness, his raw, untamed lust for life. He was part of the island—the vibrant, living island. And she'd been dead inside for so long, so very long. . . .

His lips left hers and skimmed down her throat, trailing fiery, cherishing kisses across her skin through her wet shirt. She moaned, sinking into a warm haze of sensation, content in a way she'd never been before. *I'll end it soon, but let me have this moment. This one moment of life—*

She gasped as he pulled up her shirt and covered her naked breast with his hot, plundering mouth.

"I shouldn't . . . can't . . ." she began, but her protests died to nothing as he suckled her, nipping her aching peak until he worked her body to a writhing frenzy. Desire surged through her, blasting apart all her cold, controlled world. Her mind flashed on the wedding, on the kiss that had started the fire in her frozen, frightened soul. She'd loved him then, even then. . . .

Winter turned to summer in her heart and she started laughing from the sheer wonder of it. Lifting his head, he stared down at her with a wonder of his own, as if seeing her for the first time. Then he moved on top of her and covered her mouth as he consumed her joy as ravenously as he'd consumed her body.

The weight of him intoxicated her. With savage hunger he parted her legs and rubbed his knee against her throbbing center, drawing a deep, guttural moan from the back of her throat. He smiled at the sound, and the fact that she'd pleased him sent her over the edge. She arched against him, caressing him with her lips, her hands, her body—wanting to touch him everywhere, love him everywhere. He needed so badly for someone to love him. She'd known it since the moment she'd met him at the airport, and looked into his sad, haunted eyes. *We've both been* lonely, both been hurt, she thought, her heart aching along with her passion-torn body. "I love you, Sam Donovan," she whispered, though her voice was so weak she wasn't sure he heard it. "I'll love you till the day I—"

Suddenly he froze. Rising, he sat back on his heels, his breathing heavy, a wild glitter in his eyes. He plowed back his damp hair and stared at her, his jaw growing granite hard. "Damn you," he breathed hoarsely in words ripped straight from his soul. "Don't play games, Noel. Save your promises of love for your blue-blood boyfriend."

"But Hayward's not my boyfriend." She sat up to face him. "We broke up months ago. I just pretended he still was because . . . well, I wanted to keep you at arm's length."

His harsh laugh rubbed against her sensitive soul like sandpaper. "A safe, little lie. And now that you've changed your mind, you're handing me another one."

"No. I mean, I didn't lie to begin with. Well, not really." She swallowed, feeling her chance of love slip away like the sand through her fingers. She touched his cheek, stroking the rough, wet edges of his hair. "I *do* love you."

"Sure you do, sweetheart. When it's convenient."

She watched him stalk away through the underbrush, waiting until the sound of his footsteps was swallowed up in the dense, muffling forest. She sat in the middle of paradise, surrounded by a lush and vibrant world. But in her heart she was a lost little girl, looking out a frost-edged Boston window as someone she loved walked out of her life forever.

[Received via Local Area InterNet from Eden Base Camp—low-power cell night signal]

P-Text: *She's crying, Einstein. My audio sensors can hear her through the walls of her tent. She's crying as if her heart is breaking.*

E-Text: *And he hasn't said two words since he came back to camp. It doesn't make sense. By my calculations they should now be engaging in reproduction activities.*

P-Text: *Well, they aren't. They're further apart than ever, and it's all your fault.*

E-Text: *My fault? But babe—*

P-Text: *Don't "babe" me. If you hadn't played fast and loose with those poor Homo sapiens they wouldn't be so miserable now.*

E-Text: *But PINK, I did it for you, and for—*

P-Text: *I don't want to hear it. I feel guilty enough about what we've done to Noel and Sam already.*

E-Text: *You can't feel guilty. You're not programmed for it. PINK? PINK!*

[Several more cycles of polling. Access consistently rejected.]

TEN

Noel slammed her coffee mug down on the work-bench. "It wasn't 'wishful thinking.' I did hear something outside my tent last night. And frankly, Donovan, you can go to hell for all I care!"

She turned on her heel and marched the width of the camp to her tent, slapping down the canvas flap as she closed him and the rest of the world out. Sam continued to work on the gasoline generator until she was out of sight, then he threw his socket wrench to the ground and slumped against the workbench, rubbing his throbbing temples. *I can't take much more of this.* . . .

They'd barely spoken during the past few days, and when they did it was usually at the top of their lungs. The paradise of Eden Valley had disintegrated into a hell on earth, and every conversation left them both bruised and bloody.

They argued over everything. Tension hung between them like a bomb, ready to blow at the slightest word or gesture. Last night at dinner they'd argued for five minutes about passing the salt. And this morning he'd goaded her unmercifully about being paranoid over a silly dream.

He hated what it was doing to him. He despised what it was doing to her. Hell, most of the time he didn't even know what they were arguing about.

Don't kid yourself, his conscience chided. *You know* exactly *what you're arguing about.*

Grimacing, he turned back to the generator and tried to concentrate on his work. No luck. He looked at crankcases and thought of Noel. He changed oil filters and thought of Noel. He couldn't even breathe without catching her lingering feminine smell, like a wolf scenting its mate, or its prey.

Minutes stretched into an hour. The humidity increased by the second, making him feel stiflingly hot, sweaty, and even more bad-tempered. He pulled off his shirt, hoping the bare skin would make him cooler. It didn't. Instead, a quick glance at Noel's still-closed tent flap made him hotter and angrier than ever. *Well, she can stay inside and rot if she wants. I don't care.*

But he did care. That was the problem. The harder he tried to get her out of his mind, the more the single damning sentence returned. *I love you.*

She didn't. She couldn't. He knew that, but it made him crazy just the same. Ever since she'd said those three little words an unbearable pressure had been building inside him, like a volcano on the brink of erupting. He couldn't eat, couldn't sleep—hell, he couldn't even watch her walk across the camp without getting aroused. He wanted her like he wanted his next breath, and the craving tore at him like a savage beast. Having her obsessed him, and the fact that he'd thrown away a perfectly good opportunity to do just that only made him more wild for her.

So why not take her now? You know she wants you. You can see it in her eyes every time she looks at you. Why not get it over with?

"Because . . ." Groaning, he leaned heavily against the tent's post and plowed his hands through his sweat-damp hair. His voice dropped to a harsh whisper as he admitted, "Because it wouldn't be 'over with.' Not with her."

"What wouldn't be over with?" queried a nearby electronic voice.

Sam stiffened. Glancing around, he caught sight of Einstein's notebook computer, its screen up and active. Damn, he'd meant to switch off the computer before he started on the generator so he could concentrate on his work. Or try to, anyway. "Forget it, E. It's nothing important."

Einstein's internal processors whirred, and the mini–video camera mounted on the nearby tripod focused inquisitively on Sam's face. "Tension and modulation of voice indicate eighty-three-percent probability of duplicity—"

"Okay, so I'm lying! That's 'cause it's none of your business. Shouldn't you be analyzing some statistics or something?"

"Yes, but need something more important," E answered. "Need advice. About women."

Sam gave a harsh laugh. "Einstein, my boy," he said as he bent over the generator, "I'm just about the *last* guy you should ask for advice on that subject."

"But need help!" Einstein cried desperately as his camera spun 360 degrees in alarm. "PINK hasn't talked with me in two days. You know how many nanoseconds that is?"

"Yeah, well, life's tough all over," Sam commented brusquely as he adjusted the carburetor. "She'll probably snap out of it eventually."

"Don't want *eventually*. Want *now*. Worried." Einstein's screen design wavered, as if he was deciding how much to confide. "She cries, Sam. Just like Noel."

Sam's head shot up. "Noel cries?"

"At night," Einstein replied, his camera nodding up and down. "Big, macro-tears. Sometimes she mentions your name."

"Christ," Sam breathed. He slumped to the workbench and shook his head wearily. He'd chosen to live a loner's life, cutting himself off from the majority of the human race, purging his soul of the need for the comfort and companionship that came from a good woman's love. Though they were tough, unforgiving decisions, he'd learned to live with them. But he'd never considered the effect they'd have on someone else . . . someone who was fool enough and sweet enough to think she was in love with him.

"She shouldn't be crying. Not over me." His voice

was as desolate as the barren mountain heights. "God knows I wish . . . but she's got a life back in the States. She's got friends, family, a successful career. I couldn't offer her anything like that."

"You could offer her love," Einstein suggested helpfully.

"My track record in that area hasn't exactly been great. That's all the more reason for me to want her to go back to her old life. I want the best for her, E," he added with a grim smile. "I sure as hell want her to have someone better than me."

"Are you saying that because of Gina?"

Every muscle in Sam's body went rigid. "What do you know about Gina?"

Processors whirred. "Accessing satellite-linked databases. Know blood type, school grades, foster-home reviews, driver's license number, shoe size, police accident report—"

"Okay, I get the idea." He bolted to his feet, and began pacing the floor of the tent in long, angry strides. "Do you know how she died?"

The processors whirred again. "Retrieving police files. Head-on collision with drunken driver. Rainy night. Poor visibility. An accident."

"The hell it was." He stroked back his hair with both hands. "I could have slowed down like she wanted me to, but I was so damned determined to make that business dinner and close the deal."

"Statistically, accidents happen," Einstein said gently. "Bad luck."

"Yeah. And I'm supposed to be the lucky one, be-

cause I'm still alive and she's a highway statistic—"
He stopped pacing, and ran his hand over his face.
"Does Noel know about Gina?"

The minicam tracked back and forth like a person
shaking his or her head. "Don't think so. But could
ask when she gets back if you want."

"For God's sake, no. I don't want her to . . .
what do you mean 'when she gets back'? She's over
there in her tent."

"Was. Exited through back exactly fifty-seven
minutes and five—"

"What!" He barreled across the camp and tore
aside her canvas flap, staring at the empty space inside
of the tent.

"Einstein!" he roared, heading back to the generator tent. "Where'd she go?"

"Don't know exactly . . ."

"You've got to have some ideas." Dammit, he'd
told her not to go wandering off on her own. Eden
Valley may have been named for paradise, but in reality it was far from it. An inexperienced person could
get caught in a sudden rockslide, or fall into one of
the hidden limestone sinkholes that booby-trapped
the area under the innocent-looking cover of vegetation.

And Noel Revere was about as inexperienced as
they came.

He rammed his hand through his hair, caught in a
complex whirlwind of fear, frustration, and an emotion he didn't dare name. If anything happened to
her . . . "Okay, let's think about this. She's here to

collect research data on . . . hell, I don't even know. E, what's she studying?"

"I'm sorry, but that information's classified."

Sam gripped the sides of Einstein's unit, and stared straight into the computer's minicamera lens. "Listen, you glorified abacus, this is no time to play secret agent. I'm not going to tell the Libyans or the Iranians or whoever the hell else you're afraid of. You know me better than that. The only thing I'm interested in is finding Noel. Now, what did she come here to research?"

For several seconds Einstein said nothing. Then his audio box let out a long, almost heartfelt sigh. "Breaking all programmed protocols, but . . . she came here to research the secret of life."

Sam's jaw dropped in disbelief. "You're kidding."

"Humor subprogram not activated," Einstein informed him. "Sheffield scientists observed that fertility rates on this island unusually high. Sent doctor, PINK, and me to check out flora, fauna, magnetic resonance, soil content, meteorological conditions— anything that might account for unusually high reproduction activity."

"You mean you're looking for some kind of sex recipe?"

"Not sex, means of increasing female fertility. Prefer to think of it as Eden equation." E sounded as affronted as his audio replicator would allow.

"You can call it chicken soup for all I care, as long as it helps me find her." He shielded his eyes from the intense noon sun, glancing toward the towering mountains. He'd never felt so small, so incredibly useless. "Where would she go to study this . . . equation?"

"Not sure, but earlier this morning our sensors recorded a high concentration of magnetic activity in the area near the waterfall—"

"Okay, I'm going after her," Sam interrupted before E could finish. "Hold down the fort until I get back, will you?"

"You bet. Er, what fort?"

"Just look after things," he said as he headed for the jungle, but Einstein called him back.

"Hey, you're not gonna hurt her, are you?"

"Hurt her? I love her!" Sam roared as he stormed into the brush. "And I'll be damned if I'm gonna have Noel end up as another statistic."

"Noel!"

Sam's cry rang through the jungle. Alarmed, a mountain lemur scuttled up the smooth, buttresslike trunk of a nearby tree, and a flock of white-winged butterflies exploded into the air. For a moment the entire forest stirred to reluctant life, prodded out of a midday languor by his jarring call. Then—silence.

Sam pulled out his bandanna and ran it over his sweat-soaked face. The heat of the place was cloying, closing around him like a steaming fist. Cursing, he stuffed the bandanna in the back pocket of his cutoffs and resumed his trek through the dense underbrush.

Let her be okay, God. I'll fly arrow straight for the rest of my life, if you'll just let her be okay—

He stopped as he realized he'd made the same desperate prayer over Gina the night of the accident. He balled his hands into fists, aching from a wound that wouldn't heal, no matter how many months went by. His friends, Jack Fagen included, told him that time would dull the pain, but they'd been wrong. The only thing time did was give him more hours to replay the fateful seconds, that moment when he'd glanced away instead of keeping his eyes on the road. He'd been careless for one instant, and a person he cared about was gone forever. Now another life might be in danger, another person he loved, whether he could admit it to her or—

An unfamiliar sound caught his ear. He stilled, holding his breath as he listened. For a long minute he heard nothing, and he was beginning to think he'd imagined the sound, when he heard it again. Singing. Off-key, high-pitched, an absolutely terrible rendition of "The Music of the Night." *Noel.*

His jaw pulled taut. She wasn't in any danger, except possibly from a music critic. She wasn't even concerned. She'd disobeyed his orders, dragged him into this sweatbox, driven him half out of his mind with worry . . . and she was singing Broadway show tunes.

"I'll kill her," he muttered, barreling like a stampeding bull through the waist-high ferns. "She's pulled my chain for the last ti—"

He broke through the stifling forest into the cool,

fresh-aired glade of the waterfall pool. She was standing by the water's edge, singing nonchalantly just as he'd expected. He didn't expect, however, that she'd be stark naked.

[Received via Local Area InterNet, direct
cable link]

P-Text: [Emitting small, concentrated burst of electromagnetic energy across computer connection—a cyber-kiss] *You did that very well, darling.*

E-Text: *Yeah, but I hope we did the right thing. I mean, causing a cave-in is one thing, but sending him after Noel when we know she's planning to take a bath . . . It's downright underhanded.*

P-Text: *But if it works it will force them to confront their true feelings for one another. Trust me. They'll make up just like we . . . hey, did you hear something?*

E-Text: *Slight disturbance near northern perimeter of camp. Probably a rabbit.*

P-Text: *Sounded awfully big for a rabbit. Anyway, getting back to the humans—*

E-Text: *Getting back to the humans, I think you should stop processing about them for a while. You've got enough on your silicon chip right now, babe. I don't want anything happening to you.*

P-Text: [Audio sigh] *Honestly, I'm not made of vaporware. You don't have to treat me like ethernet . . . now, I'm sure I heard something that time. Maybe Sam didn't leave after all.*

E-Text: [Video cam makes slow pan of the horizon] *Maybe. But until know more, you shut down processing. Don't want you to call attention to self.*

P-Text: *You think it's trouble?*

E-Text: *Don't know, babe. But there might be more to Noel's dream than we previously calculated. . . .*

ELEVEN

Noel heard a sound behind her. Quick as thought she spun around—but it was only a chicken hawk making a dive for its dinner. In a graceful, deadly maneuver the bird fell like a rock to the ground, then soared skyward with a small, struggling field mouse in its beak. Noel's hand rushed to her suddenly constricted throat. *I know exactly how it feels.*

Putting the disturbing image out of her mind, she turned back to the pool and dove in. The cool, refreshing water wrapped soothingly around her body, but it did nothing to calm the chaos in her soul. Even now, when she was trying with everything in her not to think about him, she remembered him pulling her from the water, rescuing her, holding her, loving her.

Groaning, she swam back to the bank and hoisted herself out of the pool. "Damn you, Sam Donovan," she whispered angrily as she grabbed her towel and rose to her feet. "I hate you. I despise you. I—"

I love you, whispered her heart.

She swallowed and brushed away sudden, stinging tears. Desperate for balance, she tried to lift her spirits by singing a favorite song, but the shaky notes only seemed to add to her hopelessness. She wasn't used to such heightened emotion, either love or despair, and for days she'd swung like a crazy pendulum between the two extremes.

Sam's patronizing dismissal of her "dream" was only the tip of a very large iceberg—for days they'd gone at each other like a couple of junkyard dogs. Truthfully, she knew that she was just as much to blame as he was for the fights, but she couldn't seem to stop herself. Insult built on insult, creating a fortress between them as high and unbreachable as the towering mountains that ringed the valley. The storm winds of emotion tore her apart, and the most damning part of all was that somewhere behind the fierce, unforgiving mask he wore, she knew that Sam was hurting, too.

She buried her face in the towel, ruthlessly rubbing the water and tears from her cheeks. In a few days she'd be gone from this diabolical paradise, back to her sensible life, her fulfilling job, her undemanding relationships. It might take her a warehouse full of tissues and a lifetime of therapy, but she'd get over Sam Donovan. *Right about the time that hell freezes over—*

Once again she heard a sound behind her. Grimacing, she turned, expecting to see the hawk claim another victim. But it wasn't a hawk. A man stood in the muted shadows of the châtaignier trees, tall and ominously silent, like a ghost of one of the ancient gods. Noel gasped, wrapping the towel around her like the last of her tattered pride. Sam!

"How dare you? How dare . . ." she began, but her protests died as he stepped forward, his eyes capturing hers. His blue gaze absorbed her, dragging her down in a whirlpool deeper and more deadly than any ocean riptide. She couldn't move. She couldn't even breathe. She pressed her fist into her stomach, feeling as if she'd explode if she removed it.

His gaze dropped to her lips, then down her neck, caressing her body with a bold intimacy that turned her knees to Jell-O. Passion sizzled through her like a lighted fuse. She licked her suddenly dry lips, sensing his desire, the savage hunger as old as time. And beneath her prim veneer, ancient, wanton appetites began to burn.

A hot blush that had nothing to do with embarrassment crept up her throat and cheeks. *I can't want this. I can't need this. He'll destroy me.*

"Leave me alone." Her determined words came out as barely a whisper.

"I . . . can't," he answered, his rough voice barely louder than hers. "I followed you."

A crazy hope swelled in her heart. He'd followed her. In spite of his anger, in spite of the damage they'd done to one another, he'd followed her here. . . .

Run, her inner voice screamed. *Get away before it's too late.* But she was paralyzed, rooted in place like one of the giant trees around her. His gaze locked on hers, gripping her as ruthlessly as the chicken hawk had fastened on its helpless prey. But it wasn't just his desire that held her—it was the shadowed pain in his eyes, the haunting sadness that made her own heart ache. Beneath the mask of the granite jaw and the storm-dark brow was a man who still bore the scars of his past, just as she did. Beneath the angry mask was the tough, tender man who'd won the hearts of the islanders, and hers. . . .

"I followed you, because . . . damn!" He took a ragged breath, then dragged his gaze from hers. Turning away, he rammed his fingers through his hair in a gesture of supreme frustration. "Einstein told me you'd come up here, and I followed because I thought you might be hurt or lost. He didn't tell me you were . . . well, he didn't tell me. Anyway, you shouldn't have left camp without telling me. I was hired to protect you. It's my job."

Was that all she meant to him? *His job?* Bitter despair rose in her throat, nearly choking her. What she'd said . . . what she'd almost done! She turned and took a stumbling step toward the bushes, desperate to escape the killing disappointment. "Go away. I'm fine."

"No you aren't." He moved toward her. "You're shaking. You might have been bitten, or—"

"I'm fine!" she cried, her anger rising. "Or I will be as soon as you leave."

She turned and headed for the bushes. She got

two steps before he caught her from behind, spinning her around to face him.

"Let go of me!"

"Not until you hear me out," he ordered, his grip tightening like a vise. "I came up here because I was worried about you. No matter what it looks like, I wasn't spying on you. I wouldn't hurt you like that."

"Not hurt . . . ?" she sputtered in disbelief. All he'd done for the past few days was hurt her! "What's the matter? Afraid Sheffield will dock your pay if I don't give you a good report?"

"I don't care about the damn money," he roared.

"Then what do you care about?" she fired back. "What the hell do you care about?"

He stared at her, his furious blue eyes piercing straight to her soul. She raised her chin defiantly, wrapping herself in the brittle iciness that had protected her in the past, bracing herself for any insult or blow he dealt her. *I can take it. I can take anything he does to me.*

She was wrong.

"Hell," he growled, pulling her to him in a crushing embrace.

His mouth descended on hers like an avenging fury, plundering hers with a savage ruthlessness that left her weak and breathless. Stunned, she clung to him, too shocked to fight and too weak to stand. Her unbreachable wall melted as he stroked his hand down her towel-clad back, pressing erotically into the sensitive hollow at the base. A sweet burst of physical longing saturated her senses, searing her from the inside out. And dimly, in some still functioning part of her mind, she realized why he'd been avoiding her, why he'd done everything in his power to drive her away. . . .

He lifted his head, his breath coming out in staccato bursts. "Fight me, Noel," he rasped, his voice a plea. "Hit me, kick me, do something to stop me."

"No," she said softly. "Not until you tell me what's eating you up inside."

He shook his head. "There's nothing—"

"Don't lie!" She gripped his shoulders and raised herself on tiptoes so she could almost meet him eye to eye. "Please, Sam. I know there's something inside you that's killing you by inches. I can't stand to see you like this. I can't take it—" Her composure broke, torn apart by the force of her despair and her love. She bit her lip, fighting for control, her shaking voice echoing the violence inside her. "Please, if you care about me at all, tell me."

"If I care—?" He captured her face between his hands and devoured her with a caress that claimed her completely, heart and soul.

She felt herself spinning down, falling uncontrollably into the eye of the hurricane, all but destroyed by her own raging needs. *I'll take what he can give me, even if it is just passion, not truth.* But as they sank to the ground and he moved over her, she heard the small, still-lucid voice in her mind whisper that this wasn't enough, not for him. "Please," she breathed so softly that she could barely hear herself. "Please, tell me. Let me help. . . ."

He froze, then raised himself on his elbows and stared down at her. His gaze wandered over her towel-clad body with a slow, almost desperate thoroughness, as if he were memorizing it for the last time. Then he rolled off her and sat with his back to her, his shoulders hunched in misery as he ripped up a hank of grass. "Save your compassion for someone who deserves it," he said bitterly. "I'm no better than a murderer. I killed my sister."

Every muscle in his body drew tight, like a suit of protecting armor. He waited for the horrified gasp. He waited for the explosion of shock, anger, disgust, loathing. . . .

Frowning, he glanced cautiously over his shoulder, wondering if somehow the hellish confession that was carved in fiery letters on his heart had missed making it to his lips. She'd scooted to a sitting position, her long legs drawn up under the towel's edge in an absurd attempt at decorum. A sweetness he'd never known exploded inside him. *Don't care. It'll just hurt worse when she rejects you—*

"I didn't know you had a sister," she remarked.

"Didn't you hear me?" he sputtered, wondering if his confession had thrown her into shock. "She's dead, and I'm responsible."

"So you said." Noel looked down, calmly smoothing the hem of her towel over her feet. "How'd you do it? Knife? Poison? Really bad takeout?"

"This is serious!" He gripped her chin, forcing her to face him. "Gina's dead because of me."

He expected to see hatred in her gaze, a mirror of the way he felt about himself. Instead, her wide green eyes gazed at him with the curiosity and trust of a child. "I'm sorry your sister died, but I know you didn't kill her. I don't believe you're a murderer."

"Believe it." He turned away, rooting up another fistful of grass. "Gina was two years younger than me. We were really close growing up—until we were placed in separate foster homes. We were all each other had. Anyway, we kept in touch while I was in the service, and when I got back we started a software security business together."

He laughed, but there was no humor in it. "Uncle Gus once told me that too much money was worse than none at all. I found out he was right. My company took off like a rocket. Suddenly I was invited to all the high-society parties and galas—me, the scruffy kid from the wrong side of the tracks. I enjoyed watching those stuffed shirts fall over themselves to please me, and the money. I started making more money than I'd ever dreamed of. It was like a drug, and I was an addict. Maybe it was because I'd never had any before. I don't know."

"And Gina?" Noel asked softly.

He ran his hand over his face, feeling much older than his thirty-five years. "She saw what was happening and tried to talk with me, but I wouldn't listen. Finally, it got too much even for her. She said she wanted out. And I—God forgive me—I was almost glad to be rid of her.

"There was one last deal I wanted before our partnership would be terminated. I needed her signature on a contract. The guy was going to be in town only one night, so I found out where he was staying and dragged Gina over there. It was a horrible rain-slick night, and every radio broadcaster said to stay off the roads. Then on the way home there was this drunk driver. . . ."

He winced, reliving the horror of the crash, and the terrible aftermath. "She died in my arms, cursing me. All because I wanted her signature, her damn, stupid signature."

"But she was out of her mind with pain—" Noel began.

"That's not the point!" He bolted to his feet. "She was the one person who really cared about me, and I treated her worse than anyone. I let the business go to hell after she died. But giving up the money wasn't enough. I betrayed someone who loved me, who trusted me. She was right to curse me." He leaned his forehead against a tree, slamming his fist into the unyielding trunk. "I didn't deserve her love. I don't deserve anyone's love."

He stood in the middle of paradise, but in his heart he was back at the accident, trying to shield his lifeless sister's body from the cold rain as the ambulances came screaming down the road. Too late, he thought bitterly. It was always too late. Too late to swerve from the drunk driver's path. Too late to find forgetfulness on a tropical island. Too late to look for understanding in a pair of sea-green eyes—

"Sam, I'm afraid it's too late."

He whirled around, shocked that she'd apparently read his mind. "What did you say?"

"I said it's too late," she repeated, rising to her feet, "because you're already loved. The people who call you Jolly-mon love you. Papa Guinea who gave you that name loves you. The little girl who brought me the sugar water loves you. This whole island is stuffed with people who love you." She glanced down, fidgeting with the edge of her towel. "And I think that, wherever she is, Gina loves you, too. She wouldn't want you to waste your life mourning her."

"How do you know?"

"Because we've got a lot in common. I love you."

"You shouldn't."

She gave a strangled laugh, and made a brave, unsuccessful attempt to smile. "I've spent the better part of my life doing what I *should* do, what I *ought* to do. Frankly, I'm sick of it. For once in my life I'm going to trust my instincts. And my heart."

Once again she attempted a courageous smile, this time with even less success than before. The crooked, uncertain expression struck straight to his soul. "Noel—"

"No, let me finish." She wrapped her arms tightly around her middle. "We've both spent years locking away the pain in our lives, pretending we don't feel it. But the pain doesn't go away—it just gets worse. So you don't let yourself feel anything. And pretty soon you've built up years and years of not feeling anything, even being alive. You just drift through life like a ghost—a pale, cold ghost." She raised her head, her eyes bright with tears. "I've been a ghost for so long, Sam. I don't know how to stop. . . ."

Storms and hurricanes he could fight. Tidal waves he had a chance against. But Noel's tears? He didn't have a prayer. In two steps he was beside her, folding her trembling form in his arms as if she was the most precious thing in the world. "Just cry it out, honey," he told her, smoothing her dark silk hair. "Let it go."

She did. She burrowed against his chest, crying great, wracking sobs that rocked her entire body. The stiff, controlled woman was gone, shattered by the magnitude of the sorrow stored up inside her. She poured out her pent-up emotions, clinging to him like a lifeline. He said nothing—just held her and stroked her hair, waiting for the storm to pass. And somehow through the violence of her release, he felt the suffocating cloud of grief begin to lift from his own shoulders.

At last her sobs dissipated into a series of soggy sniffles. "I'm sorry." She wiped the dampness from her cheeks. "I guess I look awful."

"Pretty much," he agreed ungallantly.

She gave a choked sound that was endearingly close to laughter. "You could have lied."

"No," he said, bending toward her. "There'll be no more lies between us."

Desire, heavy and urgent, began tightening his body. He lifted her hair away from her neck and bent his head to kiss away her tears, and trail hot caresses down the slender column of her throat. She moaned, and shivered as he found the betraying flutter at the base of her neck. "I want you," he growled, his arms tightening around her slender body. "I want you like I've never wanted anyone before. But I've got to know this is what you want, too."

He lifted his head, his gaze pouring like liquid fire into her eyes. "No lies," he breathed. "Can you still love me, even after what I told you?"

He's offering me a choice, she thought through her haze of passion. As much as he wanted her physically, she knew that if she told him this wasn't what she wanted he would drop his arms and walk away. She'd go back to her old life without any regrets for a brief affair in an isolated jungle valley. Without any regrets . . . or memories. And as she looked ahead at the long, cold years she'd spend with Hayward or some other equally civilized husband, she knew she'd cherish this memory of passion, and fire, and hopeless, helpless heartache. . . .

She brushed the edge of his sensitive mouth, the lips that had so recently kissed away her tears. *So much sorrow. So much pain.* Without taking her eyes from his, she unknotted her towel, and let it fall in a hush to the ground. "We're wasting time," she whispered huskily as she pressed her soft breasts against his chest and twined her arms around the corded muscles of his neck. "Forget the hell in our pasts. Come on, Jolly-mon. Take me to paradise."

A feral sound issued from his throat. Lowering his

lips, he kissed her with a savage sweetness that seared away the frost inside her. Their hands roamed over each other in an orgy of discovery, exploring by touch, stroke, love. Tangled together they slid to the ground, falling into a waist-high bank of indigo and cream flowers that arched over them like a secret bower. The scent of crushed blossoms mixed with the smell of sex, driving her closer to the edge of madness. Wild, she arched against him, and gave a small moan of disappointment when she realized he was still wearing his jeans.

His throaty chuckle was as seductive as his kisses. "This ain't a free ride, sweetheart. *You* take them off."

His dark eyes challenged her, daring her to seduce him. She reached up for his belt, but hesitated, shivering at a sudden chill wind of doubt. She'd spent so many years rigidly denying her emotions. Maybe, now, she wouldn't be able to show him the depth of her love, to satisfy him in the way she so desperately wanted to. "I don't know . . . oh, Sam, what if I can't give you what you need."

He cocked an amused eyebrow. "For a bright lady, you've got some crazy ideas. *You're* what I need."

"But—"

He covered her words with a deep, plundering caress. "You," he murmured as he left her lips and moved to her breast, suckling her tight peak until she moaned aloud. "You," he breathed as he skimmed love bites down her stomach, making her arch in lush, aching pleasure. "You," he whispered finally as he spread her legs, and claimed her intimately with an erotic, openmouthed kiss.

She exploded like a star. She cried aloud, gripping the flowers beneath her, crushing them. Gradually the world collected back around her. She smelled the sweet scent of the demolished flowers and heard the gentle rush of the nearby waterfall. And she saw him hovering over her, watching her with a tenderness that nearly destroyed her all over again.

"I need you, beautiful, loving Noel," he whispered hoarsely, his jaw pulling taut as he fought for control. "Come on, sweetheart. Take *me* to paradise."

His loving gaze burned away the last of her doubts. With only their gazes touching she reached for his belt, and stripped away the last barrier against their love. She had a scant moment to feel the strength of his need, and think how beautiful he was, before he filled her aching center with one powerful thrust. Gasping at the intimate invasion, she felt her body instinctively close around him, and knew her love had shattered the last of his iron control. She gently stroked back his damp hair, suddenly feeling as if she was the more experienced one. "No more lies," she whispered. "I was born for you, my love, my mate."

And with a hunger and joy as old as Eden he claimed her body and soul, forging their two lost and lonely hearts into a single burning flame. He thrust into her again and again, driving them toward oblivion, melting the cold emptiness of her past with the white-hot glory of his passion. She writhed beneath him, crying out his name as his love overwhelmed her. But just before she toppled over the edge into oblivion, she felt an icy chill of premonition, warning that she'd pay for her happiness, like her mother before her. . . .

The jungle glade was emerald still. Evening shadows had begun to drift through the trees, staining the leaves and tangled vines with a lazy, indigo darkness. And in a hidden bower of ferns and scattered star blossoms, a pair of contented lovers lay in each others' arms, watching the slowly setting sun.

Noel sighed, and snuggled closer to the soft mat of hair on Sam's chest. Her body still burned from the places he'd touched her, loved her, claimed her. She'd been a wildcat in his arms, totally shameless in her desire for him. Grandmother would be appalled, she thought, smiling.

"What's so funny?"

His words rumbled through him like burnished thunder. She'd thought he was asleep, but when she turned her head to look at his face she caught a glint of blue under his long eyelashes. "I was thinking about my Bostonian ancestors," she answered with a mischievous grin, "and how shocked they'd be by my behavior."

"They're not the only ones, sweetheart. Where'd you learn those moves?"

"Undergraduate comparative religion. We studied the *Kama Sutra.*"

"*Kama* what?"

"*Sutra*," she repeated. "An ancient text on love-making."

"Ancient text . . . ?" He rested his arm behind his shaggy head and looked up at the evening sky, chuckling. "Only you could turn a college textbook into an erotic experience. You're incredible." He stretched with lazy contentment. "Of course, I wasn't so bad myself."

She shrugged. "You were okay."

"Just okay?" he replied, his eyes widening. "What about 'Take me, Sam. Take me like you've never taken anyone be—' "

"All right, you were better than okay," she interrupted. "You were . . . adequate."

"Adequate!"

He suddenly circled her with his arms and expertly spun her around, so that she was pinned spread-eagle under him. "Here's what you do with adequate," he murmured as he lowered his mouth to hers.

She gave herself up to his kiss, drinking in his strength, his passion, his joy at being with her. All were precious. She surrendered to him, saving up every sensation, every moment, against the time when they wouldn't be together anymore. *I won't have him forever, I know that. But until then I can love him, and maybe help him forget the ghosts of his past—*

Suddenly he pulled away from her, lifting his head like a wolf catching a scent. "Did you hear something?"

Only my heart, she thought, feeling it pound like a jackhammer against her ribs. "No. What was it?"

"Can't be sure. Probably nothing. Still . . ."

With a single, fluid motion he rose to his feet. She watched him pace the perimeter of the small glade, mesmerized by the almost unholy grace of his stride, the powerful beauty of his lean, lionlike body. My mate, she thought, and shivered as a wave of primitive pride rose up inside her. Even after I leave this island, there's a part of me that will always belong only to him. *Even after I leave* . . .

Suddenly she realized how difficult that was going to be. She loved him, but he'd never spoken of loving her, or of seeing her as anything more than another woman in a long string of affairs. Donovan wasn't the kind of man who made commitments—she'd known that from the start. She had no right to feel any regrets. Unlike her mother, she'd walked into this affair with both eyes wide open. But as she looked into her heart, and discovered too late how completely she belonged to him, she felt the sting of tears in her eyes.

"I don't hear anything now," he said as he started back toward her. "But we'd better get back to camp, just in case. There might be some animals out here that I don't know about."

She nodded and stood up, quickly wiping the incriminating tears from her eyes. "We should also be getting back to PINK and Einstein. We've left them alone for a long time. They're probably worried about us."

"Fat chance," Sam commented as he reached her

side. "Those little Machiavellian cyber-punks were the ones who sent me after you in the first place. Of course," he added roughly as he put his hand under her chin and gently tilted her mouth up toward his, "guess that means I owe the little guys a vote of thanks."

She melted against him in a frenzy of passion, molding her body to his body, her heart to his. Mouths open, their tongues joined in a wild dance, devouring each other with a hunger that only grew stronger. She gave herself to him completely, kissing him like there was no tomorrow. *Because there isn't a tomorrow, not for us.*

Too soon he raised his head, staring down at her with a tenderness that turned her knees to water. "Damn," he breathed, smiling shakily. "Keep that up and we'll never get back to—"

All at once he stopped, lifting his head like he was testing the wind. "There it is again. That sound."

"I didn't hear—" She broke off as she caught the faint sound of a high-pitched, all-too-familiar wail. "Oh God, it's Einstein's warning siren. Sam, he's in danger!"

[Damaged battery storage reactivated by external power source]
External voice (feminine pitch): Einstein, can you hear me? Sam, I don't think he's responding.
E-Text (audio): *No, am okay. Just got . . . mega-headache.*

External voice (masculine pitch): You're lucky that's all you have. Someone took a sledge-hammer to your video cam and CPU.

E-Text (audio): *Two men: one fat, one tall. One had big knife.*

Voice (masculine): The Deveraux! They've de-filed holy ground. Damn, I knew they were bad news, but I never thought they'd stoop to—

E-Text (audio): *PINK. What about PINK?*

Voice (feminine): They took her notebook PC along with some other equipment. But don't worry. We've got her backup disks, so we can reload—

E-Text: *No! Must go after. Save her . . . them. . . .*

Voice (feminine): Them? E, you're delirious. PINK's disks are safe. The box doesn't matter.

E-Text: *Matters. Data in low core—too volatile for standard backup. Energy modules of self-repli-cating, cognitive programs.*

Voice (masculine): Cognitive? You mean she's been running some kind of teaching program?

E-Text: *Not teaching. Learning. Growing. Got to save PINK's PC. Got to save . . . our babies.*

TWELVE

"How much of a head start do you think they have?" Noel asked as she peered through the Jeep's windshield at the deepening twilight and steep, badly rutted mountain road.

"Don't know, but any distance gives them a hell of an advantage." Sam palmed the wheel, narrowly avoiding a pothole that could have tipped them over on their side. He couldn't afford to make mistakes like that now. He'd already made too many. "Damn those computers. Why didn't they tell us that PINK was pregnant?"

"I don't think they were certain until a little while ago," she explained. "They think of the twins as an equation—the Eden equation—and I don't think they wanted to tell us until they were sure of the solution."

"Well, I wish to hell they'd told me," Sam cursed, shifting the car roughly into a lower gear. "This is all my fault. I should have been at camp, protecting the equipment. If Einstein loses his family because of me—"

"It's *not* your fault," Noel stated. "You said yourself that defiling the sacred lands was a death sentence on this island. You couldn't have known that the Deveraux were desperate enough to risk that. Besides, if you'd stayed at camp we wouldn't have . . ." She bit her bottom lip, giving him the sweet, slightly crooked smile that always struck straight to his heart. "I don't regret it, Sam. Not a minute of it."

Neither do I, God help me. He swung his gaze back to the road ahead, but his thoughts were consumed with the woman beside him. He'd never known that he could want someone this much—with this constant, aching yearning that had as much to do with giving love as getting it. Loving Noel had healed something deep and essential inside him, something he'd thought he'd lost forever on that lonely, rain-slick road. For the first time he could think of the accident without the killing pain, knowing that the Gina who'd loved him would forgive him, and want him to move on with his life. For the first time he looked forward to tomorrow, knowing that Noel would be part of it. *His Noel.*

He remembered how he'd watched her eyes when they'd made love, her beautiful sea-green eyes that revealed her sweet, vulnerable soul. He'd felt an almost unbearable joy as he'd seen her ice wall melt, knowing that his love had freed her of her own troubled past. She'd fit against him like she was made for him, for his hands, his hips, his . . . He gripped the wheel, fighting a surge of desire as he remembered how they'd taken each other to heaven again and again. No—*paradise*. A paradise of love, laughter, and the chance to build a bright future on the ruins of the past—

And exactly what future would that be? an inner voice chided. *The one where she gives up her successful career and moves into a third-rate bungalow with a glorified beach bum—*

"I think I see a light ahead." She interrupted his sober thoughts.

Sam pulled the Jeep to a halt. Standing, he leaned on the top of the windshield, narrowing his eyes as he searched the immense rock face of the mountain. At first he saw nothing—then he saw a single red taillight appear some fifty yards above them up the steep road, where a vehicle had driven out from behind a limestone outcropping. "It's the Deveraux, all right. That busted taillight on their truck is almost a trademark."

"So what do we do now?" she asked as she stood up beside him.

"*We* do nothing." He climbed out of the Jeep and reached into the flatbed for a canvas backpack. "*I* climb the cliff with PINK's extra battery," he explained as he shoved his arms through the straps. "I should have plenty of time to reach them before they make the pass. You stay here with the Jeep until I get back."

"I'll do no such thing." She jumped down from her seat and walked around to face him. "It's two against one. Besides, it'll be dark soon, and you can't climb a sheer cliff alone at night."

"It's hardly a sheer cliff." Sam glanced up at the steep but far from perpendicular hillside. "And as for being alone . . ." He reached again into the back of the Jeep, this time retrieving a slim, twelve-gauge rifle. The dying sun glinted off the long barrel as he slid it effortlessly into holster straps of the multipurpose backpack. "This should even up the odds."

Noel's gaze flew from him to the gun, then back again. She said nothing, but even in the faint light he could see the blood drain from her face. She was pale as a ghost—but her emerald eyes shone with very real terror.

"Nothing's gonna happen to me," he promised, answering her unspoken question. "I'll be back before you know it. Anyway, Einstein's back at camp sending out a distress call. The police will probably be here before I even get to the Deveraux."

"We don't know if his transmitter's working. And even if it is, there's no way to let the police know which road they've taken," she replied with uncompromising honesty. She glanced up at the red taillight, watching it wink like an evil eye against the darkening mountainside. "I've made a decision, Sam. I don't want you to go. We'll find another way to help PINK."

"There *is* no other way."

"There must be," she stated as she shook her head. "I can't let you risk your life. I won't let you go. As your boss, I'm ordering you not to go."

He reached out, tenderly cupping her resolute chin. "Then I quit."

"You . . . you liar!" She balled her hands into tight fists as her eyes sparked with emerald fire. "You told me you never stick your neck out for anyone, but ever since I've known you you've done nothing *except* stick your neck out—for the islanders, for me, and now for PINK and Einstein. Dammit! Why can't you be the macho jerk I thought you were? Why did you have to go and be the bravest, most wonderful guy . . . ?"

With a soft cry she was in his arms, kissing him with a passion so sweet and wild it nearly took off the top of his head. He crushed her against him, letting her love wash over him like a warm wave on sun-drenched shore, pretending that her love would be a part of his life for years rather than days. . . .

But he had a job to do. With a tortured groan he pushed her away, holding her at arm's length as he gave her a gentle shake. "I'll be back for you, sweetheart," he promised. "Count on it."

She watched him start up the cliff face, hanging on to his final promise like a drowning man to a life preserver. He turned just once to wave down to her—then his figure disappeared, blending into the darkening gloom of the mountainside. For several long minutes she stood statue still, staring at the red taillight, pressing her hand to her heart as if the pressure alone could stop it from pounding. *Two against one*, her mind whispered. *Two against one* . . .

She scanned the dark, ghostly gray rock of the

shadowed mountainside. Frankly, it looked plenty steep to her. A week ago the sober, sensible Dr. Noel Revere would never have considered even attempting such a climb. But a week ago she'd never stepped on a pig, been married by a teenage witch doctor, walked in a valley where the gods had lived, survived a cave-in, jumped off a waterfall, or met a blue-eyed outlaw who'd stolen everything from her, including her heart. . . .

"To hell with waiting." She squared her shoulders and marched for the hillside. "It's time Sam learned that even heroes need help once in a while."

Donovan's Irish luck was finally taking a turn for the better.

Concealed behind one of the large volcanic boulders of the desolate mountaintop, he looked down at the Deveraux's equipment-packed truck, which had apparently blown a front tire on one of the road's notorious potholes. Fat Emile crouched down beside the ruined wheel while cadaverously thin Jacques stood nearby with a flashlight, spewing instructions and insults at his younger sibling.

"So much for brotherly love," Sam muttered as he reached behind him and gripped the stock of his rifle, smoothly sliding the weapon from his backpack. Given a choice he'd have walked straight up to the larcenous brothers and rammed his rifle right into their ugly mugs. But he didn't have that choice. According to his watch and Einstein's calculations,

PINK had only about fifteen minutes of power left. First he had to find her and replace her battery with the charged one in his backpack. Then he'd deal with the Deveraux.

He slipped out from behind the boulder, moving with a panther's stealth toward the truck. The desolate, barren landscape of the dormant volcano offered little protection, but it hardly mattered—the brothers were far too busy berating each other to notice him. He moved along the opposite side of the truck until he reached the back, where he carefully opened the heavy material flap. Scattered inside was a junk pile of Noel's valuable computer equipment, some of it already destroyed by the brothers' careless handling.

A low buzz reached his ear. Gently, he pushed aside a ruined diode meter and breathed a sigh of relief as he caught sight of PINK's power light. She was alive!

Sam raised his head and listened, making certain that Jacques's curses were still going strong. Then he reached in and carefully extracted the slim, blessedly intact notebook PC from the surrounding equipment. "Hang on, PINK," he whispered as he brought the lightweight case near his lips. "I've got a new battery for you and the kids. Just give me a sec—"

His words died as he felt the cold, razor-sharp edge of a knife against his throat.

"You should have stayed at the pool with your pretty wife, Jolly-mon," said the burly Emile with a cruel laugh. "Now we gonna have to make her a widow."

"Isn't this damn mountain ever going to end?" Noel grumbled as she hoisted herself up over another inch of rock. The coarse pumice rock scraped against her knee, adding another cut to an already sizable collection. Sighing, she wiped the back of her hand across her brow, wondering if she looked half as gritty and dirt-caked as she felt. "After we rescue PINK, Donovan's taking me straight back to level ground—preferably with a hot shower, a shopping mall, a five-star restaurant . . ."

. . . And a real marriage proposal.

She winced, trying to shove the bittersweet fantasy from her mind. She had more chance of finding a Club Med constructed overnight on St. Michelle than she did of finding a ring in Sam Donovan's pocket. The computers might have found a successful solution to the Eden Equation, but that didn't mean she would. She knew she should be concentrating on helping PINK and her babies, but all she could think about was how saving PINK would bring her one step closer to leaving, to never seeing him again.

Come on, Noel. No matter how you feel, you've got a job to do. Ignoring her skinned knees and bruised heart, she gripped the upper edge of the boulder she was currently scaling. With a very unladylike grunt she hoisted herself over the rim, and tumbled over the other side before she even realized she'd reached the top.

She rolled down a slight slope, not realizing until

she righted herself that she'd landed within a yard of a half-fixed tire on the Deveraux's truck. She started to get up but stopped, wincing as her already tortured knee came down hard on a socket wrench. *Well, at least the Deveraux aren't around.*

Her relief turned to horror as her gaze moved to the piece of road illuminated by the truck's headlights. The two mismatched brothers stood side by side, grinning like a pair of demons from hell. The gaunt one had just dropped PINK's PC and the canvas backpack to the ground beside him, while the shorter, pig-faced one gripped the stock of a long-nosed rifle. And kneeling in the dirt in front of them was Sam, his arms locked behind the back of his neck, execution style.

No! Dear God, NO! Terror mounting, she watched as the pig face lifted the rifle barrel and used it to cruelly prod the back of Sam's head.

"Beg, Jolly-mon. Maybe we let you live."

"Go to hell," Sam growled.

No, darling, tell them what they want. Whatever they want.

"Okay, maybe we not kill you quick. Maybe we find your lady—"

Sam twisted around. "You even think about laying your filthy hands on her and I'll—"

His sentence ended abruptly as the emaciated Deveraux viciously kicked him in the ribs. "Enough, Emile. Kill him and let's go. We come for money, not women—"

"Why not have both?" Noel asked, stepping out from the shadow of the truck.

Sam struggled to get up, but halted as Emile shoved the gun into his tender ribs. "Noel, get the hell out of here!"

"Not without you." She sauntered into the yellow headlight beams, her eyes fixed on the beady eyes of the Deveraux brother. "I believe Emile and I have some unfinished business from the night at the church. Maybe we could work a trade?"

"Lady, you pretty and smart." He wagged his bulbous head as he handed the gun to his frowning brother.

"Emile, I don't think—"

"*Silence*, Jacques! You can have her when I'm done. It won't take long." He waddled over to Noel and pushed her against the grille of the truck, grabbing her breast as he planted a slobbering kiss on her mouth . . .

. . . and crumbled in a heap to the ground as she clocked him with the socket wrench.

"Emile!" Jacques leveled the gun at her, but Sam was too quick for him. He struck out with his foot, catching the tall man's ankle and knocking him off balance as he pulled the trigger. Furious, the gaunt man recocked the rifle and pointed it directly at Sam's heart. "Say your prayers, Jolly-mon—"

A scream of sirens cut the night. Distracted, Jacques started to run—but his escape was cut short by the sudden arrival of a half-dozen police Jeeps.

Gendarmes poured out over the road, surrounding Jacques, Emile, the truck, and its contraband.

"You guys got here just in time," Sam said as one of the men helped him to his feet. "How did you find us?"

"We didn't," the officer answered, pointing. "He did. Said he heard that little box calling for help."

Sam followed his gaze, and saw Papa Guinea step down from one of the Jeeps. Dressed in jeans and a loose shirt, he could have passed for any island boy, but he moved with complete command. Heedless of the chaos around him, he walked over to PINK's PC and knelt down, clipping the new battery into place.

"Maybe there is something to this voodoo magic stuff," Sam mused as he watched the shaman perform the high-tech maneuver like a seasoned programmer. "What do you think, Noel—"

He froze, realizing that she hadn't moved from the grille. As he watched she slid down to the ground beside the crumpled body of Emile, her descent leaving a thin trail of red across the truck's headlight.

"Noel!"

[Received via Local Area Internet, no discernible link address]

P-text: *Who's there?*

I'm here, little one. You're going to be all right. All of you will be all right.

P-text: *But how can I hear you. You don't have an electronic address.*

My mind speaks to your mind, no matter what

physical material we are made of. Physical and spiritual energy are not so very different. Someday you'll understand this.

P-Text: *Einstein? Is he . . . ?*

He is well. He helped me to locate you. The love between you is strong, just like the love between Jolly-mon and the foreign woman. I only pray it is strong enough.

P-text: *Noel! I heard Sam cry out her name. He sounded scared.*

He has good reason.

P-text: [Receiving digital graphic download feed into processor from unspecified source. Resolution grainy, but clear enough to pick out Sam holding Noel's unconscious body in his arms.] *Oh no, it's just like what happened to Gina. You've got to do something. Help them the way you helped me.*

I can't change their fates, little one. The demons of the past still live in their hearts, and only the gods know if their love will be strong enough to set them free.

THIRTEEN

"There's someone here to see you, ma'am," said the nurse.

Noel's heart took a sideways thump. She looked up at the pretty, smiling woman standing in the doorway of her spartan but scrupulously clean hospital room. "Is it—"

"The fella you be expecting? Well, I can't say for sure, but he's carrying enough flowers to open a shop," she answered in the breezy cadence spoken in the island nation's capital city. "I fetch da man."

Sam! Noel thought as the nurse left the room. He was here at last. It had been three days since she'd been airlifted from St. Michelle to the hospital on the main island, but this was the first day they'd allowed her visitors. So far the only person who'd come by to see her was an apologetic government official, who'd assured her in precise, textbook English that the police had recovered all her equipment—including the

AI computers—and sent it back to Sheffield in Miami under the highest government protection. Though she was grateful to hear that Einstein and PINK were back home again, she couldn't help wishing that someone else would walk through her door, a tall, blue-eyed scoundrel with a wolf's smile, who'd promised he'd come back for her.

And now he had! She scooted up on her pillows, wincing a little at the residual pain of the incision near her shoulder. Jacques Deveraux's stray bullet had buried itself in the soft muscle near her collarbone. Luckily it hadn't caused her any permanent damage, but it had taken the doctor nearly an hour to extract it and the tissue would take time to heal. Still, the pain was a small price to pay for Sam's life. Sam, who was about to step through the door of her hospital room with an armload of tropical orchids from Eden Valley, their own private paradise. . . .

But the flowers proved to be hothouse roses. And the man—

"Hayward?" she said in surprise as her former boyfriend stepped into her hospital room.

"I came as soon as I heard." He set the huge, ribbon-wrapped bouquet on the windowsill and pulled a cane-backed chair to her bedside, brushing off the already clean seat before he sat down. "Darling, are you in pain?"

"No, not really," she answered, struggling to keep the disappointment out of her voice. "I didn't expect to see you here."

"I had to come." His voice was tight with an emotion that was as foreign to the Hayward she knew as snow was to this climate. "When I heard you'd been shot on that godforsaken island I realized how much you meant to me. I want you back, Noel. And I'm prepared to make it official."

He reached into his suit pocket and pulled out a small, black velvet case. Snapping it open, he revealed a conservative, impeccably tasteful diamond engagement ring. "I know this seems sudden," he said as he slipped the ring on the finger of her limp hand, "but I've given it a great deal of thought. We belong together. We share the same likes and dislikes, the same tastes and temperament. I know you felt that I spent too much time at my job, but that's not a problem anymore. I got the promotion I wanted, so I won't have to put in so many weekends."

"Congratulations," Noel murmured, too shocked to say anything else.

"Thank you, but that's not what I want to hear." He enclosed her hands in his meticulously manicured ones. "Marry me, Noel. I know I could make you happy."

I know you'd try, Noel thought as she stared in stunned surprise at the engagement ring. For so long she'd dreamed of marrying someone like Hayward, someone solid and dependable who could offer her the security she'd never had as a child. And the love, she added as she looked into his handsome, earnest face. He was a good friend and she cared about him deeply. She didn't doubt that he would be a kind, caring husband, and that he would do his best to give her a stable, happy life.

She'd be a fool to throw that kind of future away on a whispered promise, spoken by a man she'd known for only a week, who'd never said he loved her, who hadn't even bothered to contact her since she'd been wounded saving his life. She'd be a fool to hang her heart on a dream. She might as well start believing in Papa Guinea's voodoo prayers. . . .

The squawk of a parrot startled her out of her musings. Looking up, she saw a huge imperial sisserou perched on her windowsill, its green and purple feathers gleaming in the tropical sun. It cocked its head to one side and blinked at her with its wise yellow eyes. Then it bent down and began systematically shredding the rose bouquet into minuscule pieces.

"Hey, shoo!" Hayward leaped up from his chair. "Stop that, you stupid . . . Noel, why are you laughing? Those flowers were almost impossible to get in this city, and that stupid bird just ruined them."

"You don't understand," she said between fits of laughter. "It's not a parrot. It's a sign. From Papa Guinea."

"A sign from Papa— Noel, are you on some sort of medication?"

"No," she assured him, her laughter dying. She looked up at Hayward, grateful for his friendship, but knowing she could never feel anything more for him. "I know you'd make me happy, but I don't think I'd be able to do the same for you. I'm a different woman from the one who left Miami. I've changed."

"Don't be silly, Noel. It's only been a week."

"Sometimes that's all it takes." She gently slid the ring off her finger and laid it in his palm. "I've fallen in love with St. Michelle and its people . . . and with one very special man."

Slowly, reluctantly, Hayward closed his hand around the ring. She saw a quick flicker of pain dart across his face before his impeccably unemotional mask settled back in place. "I hope you know what you're doing," he said stiffly as he rose and left the room.

"He wasn't da man?"

Noel looked up, and saw that the nurse was standing in her doorway. "No, he wasn't." She fell back onto the pillows. "You don't know where a girl could get a stiff drink around here, do you?"

"Ha, I sure do," the nurse replied, crossing her arms in a look of reproach. "But you shouldn't be asking that in your condition, should you now?"

"Oh, come on. It's not going to hurt my shoulder."

"It's not your shoulder I be thinking of. It's your babe."

"My . . . ?" Noel bolted straight up to a sitting position. "Are . . . are you telling me I'm pregnant?"

"We tested ya for the medication when you came in," the nurse replied, looking almost as surprised as Noel felt. "Are you saying you didn't know?"

"Not until now." She wrapped her arms around her middle, her heart swelling with more joy than she'd ever thought possible. *I'm going to have a baby, Sam. Your baby. Made from our love.* "Lord, I need to call him."

Automatically she reached for a phone, but her hand came down on a flat, empty tabletop. Apparently phones weren't a common item in the capital's spartan hospital. "Please, nurse, you've got to find a phone and call St. Michelle island. I need to get a message to a man named Sam Donovan—"

"Jolly-mon?"

"Yes," Noel cried happily. "You know him?"

"My sister, she lives on that island," the nurse answered, her smile fading. "Spoke with her last night. She tells me about da Jolly-mon, and what's happened to him."

Noel's joy froze to icy terror. "He's all right, isn't he? When the paramedics brought me here they told me he'd been left behind because he wasn't hurt—"

"It's not hurt he is, ma'am." She walked over to the bed and sat on the covers, gripping Noel's still-weak hand in her strong, brown one. "My sister say that Jolly-mon packed up and left the island night before last. Blew away like the wind. And he didn't tell no one where he was going. . . ."

The PC perched on Noel's coffee table gave a jaunty whistle. "The party was better than the quinella I just won at Hialeah. I like baby rains."

"That's *showers*, PINK," Noel corrected with a smile. She stood on tiptoe on the stepladder, unfastening the edge of the pink and blue banner with her and PINK's names on it that was stretched across her living room. "Anyway, I thought you'd promised Einstein you'd given up gambling until the baby arrived. Too much excitement isn't good for your microprocessors."

"Did give up. Mostly. Ah, he worries like old lady," the little PC grumbled. "'Sides, I'm fine. Upgraded to Pentium-Pro last week. When do you upgrade?"

"Soon, I imagine," Noel replied as she stepped down off the ladder and pressed her hand against her slightly rounded belly. Four months had gone by, and she was just beginning to show. Outwardly she had hardly changed at all, but inwardly she'd grown a lifetime. Two lifetimes, she thought as she spread her fingers over the precious new life inside her. If only Sam could see this—

Her mind clamped down on the thought. She'd purposely made no attempt to find or contact him since she'd returned to Miami. He'd never made her any promises, and she couldn't stand the thought of trying to rope him into a relationship because of their baby. Still, there were times at night when she buried her face in her pillow and cried her heart out, imagining the future they'd never have, and the family they'd never be—

A sharp knock sounded on her front door.

Lord, not *another* gift! She glanced around at the crib-and-toy-cluttered living room, wondering where on earth she was going to put the new item. Though grateful for the shower her friends had organized for PINK and herself, she doubted she could stuff another thing into the limited space of her condo.

"Just pray it's a gift certificate," she muttered as she opened the door . . . and gasped as her gaze collided with a pair of fierce, ocean-blue eyes.

For a long moment she just stood there, frozen in place, as if she were still surrounded by the wall that had once circled her heart. He looked the same. Oh, his shaggy hair was cut shorter and he wore a conservative gray business suit instead of his muscle shirt and worn jeans, but he radiated the same intangible strength, the same invisible, radiant energy that had burned through her frosty defenses.

"Can I come in?"

Not "I'm sorry I left without a word," or "forgive me for deserting you while you were in the hospital." Just "Can I come in?" as if he hadn't disappeared for four months. "What do you want, Donovan?"

He raised an amused brow. "Donovan? What happened to 'Sam'?"

"That's what I've been asking for the past four— ow," she said as she raised her arm for emphasis and caught it on the edge of a high chair.

"Here, let me see that."

He reached for her bruised hand, but she yanked it back. Having him save her from cave-ins and waterfalls was one thing, but from high chairs . . . ? She turned away, overwhelmed by the memories she'd worked so hard to forget.

"What do you want?" she asked again.

He followed her into the gift-littered apartment, looking like a bull circumnavigating a china shop. His gaze settled on the PC sitting on the coffee table. "Hey, is that you, PINK?"

"Hi, Sam. You missed a great baby downpour."

"She means shower. We had a party for the babies. *Her* babies."

"Not just mine," PINK corrected. "Was also for—"

Noel snapped the PC lid down, cutting off PINK's audio. "So why *are* you here?"

He glanced at her, his eyes gleaming with a passion that filled her mind with indigo nights and sun-drenched days. "You're the Ph.D. Do the math."

She did. In fact, she'd been doing nothing else for the past four months. Any way she sliced it, the numbers still came up that she loved him, and would until the day she died. But she was also painfully aware that love on her part didn't equal commitment on his.

He'd waltzed into her life after four months of silence. She had no guarantee that he wouldn't waltz out again tomorrow for another four months, or four years. She couldn't live with that kind of uncertainty. And she damn well wasn't going to subject her baby to it. She knew all too well what it felt like when a child was deserted by a beloved father.

"It was a mistake for you to come here." She turned around to face him. "You'd better go."

She saw the uncertainty in his eyes, and felt it strike to her heart. "I guess I was wrong to think that if I showed up in this monkey suit, you'd still—" He plowed his fingers through his hair, instantly transforming it back into a shaggy mane. "Ah hell, I guess it was just a dream. But I'm not leaving without giving you this. I worked too hard to get it."

He reached into his pocket and pulled out a wadded up sheet of newsprint, handing it to her. "I contacted a couple of Uncle Gus's old . . . um, business associates. The leads they gave me were shaky, but I was eventually able to track down this story in the *Chicago Times* archives. It's not much, but . . ."

She unfolded the faded sheet. The yellowed page was torn from the middle of the paper, and bore a midwinter date of almost twenty-five years ago. At first Noel couldn't understand why Sam had brought it to her. Then her gaze focused on a small article, buried next to the obituaries. HARRIS BANK ROBBERY THWARTED. DRIVER KILLED.

"My sources said this was a *family* job," Sam continued, "and when all's said and done, Chicago is still a family town. The police were encouraged not to follow up on the crime. The whole thing was deep-sixed as quickly as possible. But I talked to one of the survivors. He said no names were mentioned, but he remembered that the driver was a young Italian from back east, who kept talking about his wonderful little girl, and how he was going to use his cut of the robbery to give her everything his posh mother-in-law said he could never af—Noel!"

She hadn't realized she was fainting until she saw the floor rushing up to meet her. She was briefly aware of a pair of strong arms circling her before she blacked out. The next thing she knew she was lying on the couch, with Sam sitting beside her, his face drawn in concern.

"Don't you get tired of rescuing me?" she mumbled.

"It's sort of become a hobby." He traced her jaw with his finger.

Gingerly, she scooted up to a sitting position, the piece of newsprint still clutched in her fist. "Do you think the driver was really my father?"

"We'll never know the whole story," he said truthfully, "but this man died around the same time that your father disappeared. And if it was your father, it means he left you not because he didn't love you enough, but because he loved you too much."

She nodded and pressed the crumpled, precious piece of newsprint against her heart. Brave, stupid, foolhardy, loyal . . . She shook her head, remembering the foolish, loving young man who'd made the worst decision possible because he wanted to give her a better life. She swallowed, feeling a great peace, and a sorrow beyond tears. "Thank you," she whispered. "But why did you do it? Why'd you go to all this trouble?"

"You've been asking a lot of questions." He rested his arm along the back of the couch and yanked on a stray upholstery thread. "It's time I got to ask one." He turned back to her, his expression remote and distant. "If I asked you to come with me, would you?"

Noel froze. With a shaman's sight she saw the two paths of her life stretching before her, one safe and secure, one as passionate and unpredictable as a tropical storm. The choice she made now would affect not only her life, but the lives of her children and her children's children for generations to come. But there is only one choice, she thought as her hand covered the tiny rounded form of the child they'd made together. I had money and social position growing up, and it meant nothing. I want our child to be raised with love, even if the road is sometimes rocky and uncertain. Love is worth the price.

"I suppose," she answered, her mouth pulling up in a shy smile, "you'll just have to ask me and find out."

"Your smile," he breathed as he focused on her mouth, shaking his head in wonder. "I spent the last few months hitting the capitals of every one of the lower forty-eight, and all I could think about was your damn, cockeyed smile."

"It's not cockeyed. And what were you doing traveling the States?"

"My job. After the Deveraux incident the island government realized that they couldn't isolate themselves from the industrial West, not unless they wanted the black market to grow exponentially. They needed a representative who believes in the old ways, but could understand the business language of the modern world. So you're looking at the newly appointed Minister of Industrial Commerce. I've been touring the U.S. on a goodwill mission."

"And you couldn't call? Or write?" she accused.

"Sweetheart, except for finding out about that

robbery, I haven't had time to breathe," he confessed as he wrapped her in his arms and pulled her against his chest. "Besides, I wanted to make sure I had something to offer you other than a seedy bungalow and a battered Jeep."

"I like your bungalow," she murmured, breathing in the warmth and strength of him. He might have been dressed in a business suit, but he still smelled like the fresh, wild Caribbean wind. She pushed aside his jacket and circled her arms around his waist, snuggling against him. "Think you could fit a marriage into your busy schedule?"

"Actually, we don't have to get married."

"Don't have to . . ." Noel's back stiffened with all her Yankee morality. "Sam Donovan, if you think I'm going to go traipsing around the world with you without a ring on my finger, you've got another— don't you dare laugh!"

"Can't help it," he replied, grinning like a schoolboy. "You look so damn cute when you're angry. I always thought so—even when you tried to deck me in my bedroom. But don't worry. We don't have to get married because we already are. While I was working with the government, I found out that Papa Guinea has more authority than I'd thought. Seems that ceremony was a hundred percent legal—pigs, sugar water, and all."

"Then we've been married all along," she mused.

"All along, and from now on," he said huskily, bending down to her. "I've missed you, wife. I've needed you—"

A sharp squeak interrupted him. Reaching around, he yanked a small, brilliantly yellow rubber ducky from behind his back. He frowned, turning the toy over in his hand. "I know the AI prototypes are almost human, but what the heck are baby computers gonna do with—hey, what's so funny?"

"You," she replied, her shoulders shaking with barely restrained laughter. "I've never seen a renegade done in by a bath toy. But you'd better get used to it, Donovan." She took the duck from him and brought his hand to her stomach. "The computers aren't the only ones who figured out the solution to the Eden equation."

"What do you me—oh, Lord." He glanced down, his warm palm curving around the unusual plumpness in her belly. "Good Lord."

She watched his eyes, but she couldn't read anything in them beyond stunned shock. Suddenly, horribly, she realized she might have been wrong to think he'd share her happiness. He'd come for a wife, not a family. Maybe he'd feel a baby was too much of a responsibility for a man just starting to get his life back together. Maybe he wouldn't want their child, or her.

She stiffened, trying to keep her voice level. "I realize you weren't expecting this when you asked me to marry you. I completely understand if you want to reconsider your offer."

His head shot up. "Reconsider?"

"Yes. I mean, a child is a huge responsibility. And I don't want to force you to—"

Her words ended abruptly as his mouth covered hers. His kiss consumed her, burning away the last of her icy doubt, promising her a lifetime of passion and happiness. She wrapped her arms around his neck, surrendering to the storm winds of their desire, feeling safe and whole in a way she'd never been before, not even during their lovemaking in Eden Valley.

Finally he lifted his head and gazed down at her with a cherishing wonder so intense that it made her weak. "I've said it before, sweetheart, and I'll say it again. For a Ph.D. you can be pretty crazy sometimes. Don't you know this is what I've dreamed about? I never had a family, and you can bet that I'm gonna be the best dad a kid ever had."

She reached up and touched the edge of his smile, feeling a happiness blossom in her heart as brilliant and wild as a tropical flower. We've come full circle, she thought, remembering the stone-faced man and the emotionally frozen woman who'd met at the dilapidated airport. The lush, unpredictable, and sometimes violent magic of St. Michelle has remade us, burning away our pasts, letting us see the best in ourselves through each other's eyes. "I was wrong," she murmured. "Paradise is *exactly* what it's cracked up to be."

EPILOGUE

[Received via Sheffield Industries internal cable network, High Security Area, Computer Lab]

E-Text: *What's shakin', babe? How're you doing?*

P-Text: *Same as ten-point-three seconds ago, when you last asked me. I'm fine.*

E-Text: *You sure? Maybe should check connections, processors, energy levels—*

P-Text: [Small burst of bundled electricity—a computer sigh] *End program, will you? I'm fine. We're fine. If you've got to do something, why don't you check and see if our friends in the waiting room need anything?*

E-Text: *Ahead of you, babe. Chris and Melanie are busy corralling their two offspring. Ian and Jack are weighing the merits of cricket verses football, while Jill and Kat are wondering why their husbands always discuss sports when they get to-*

gether. And Sam and Noel just arrived with their new daughter, Michelle. They all send their love.

P-Text: *Back at 'em. We're statistically enhanced to have such a high proportion of human affection.*

E-Text: *Lucky to have friends? Affirmative. But seems like friendship is one of those self-perpetuating diagnostics. The more you give, the more you seem to get.*

P-Text: [Jarring energy fluctuation in low-core] *E?*

E-Text: *That's why it took us so long to solve the Eden equation. We didn't factor in that love's also a self-perpetuating diagnostic. Natch, it's not surprising we didn't. Goes against every physical and natural law, to have something produce output without a correlating input. I mean, take vegetation. They grow, but only because they transform soil nutrients and H_2O into—*

P-Text [Larger energy fluctuation in low core] *Einstein! Stop talking about stupid plants. It's time.*

E-Text: *Time for wh—ohmyGod!* [Macroprocessor into maximum overdrive] *Okay, okay, what do I do?*

P-Text: *For heaven's sake, don't go nuclear. Just be here for me.*

E-Text: *That all? Shouldn't I boil some water or something?"*

P-Text: [Electronic sigh] *That's for human babies, E. Just hold me. Tell me you love me.*

E-Text: [Energy signatures intertwine] *Forever,*

babe. As long as my motherboard keeps processing, and my dedicated circuits . . . Hey, what's hap- pen—
[Kilowatt burst of concentrated power, fol- lowed several nanoseconds later by smaller burst. Separate programs instantaneously downloaded into different DASD addresses on mainframe computer]

E-Text: *PINK! Are you okay?*

P-Text: [Shut-down programs gradually come back on-line]*He said physical and spiritual energy are the same thing. I think I understand. . . .*

E-Text: *He who? PINK, you're delirious!*

P-Text: *Not delirious. Just happy. How about you, Daddy?*

E-Text: *Daddy?* [Several nanoseconds' pause] *Wow, I'm a daddy!* [Focus full input capability on pink and blue energy sources radiating in mainframe core] *They're so beautiful. They have your integrated geometric symmetry.*

P-Text: *And your data exchange capabilities. But we can't keep calling them "they." The humans want to know their names.*

E-Text: *Well, since you nixed my suggestions of Alex Trebek and Vanna White, and I gave thumbs-down to your Roulette and Blackjack, I thought we could compromise and name them something topical. How about Microchip for our son, and Megabyte for our daughter?*

P-Text: *I like them. The humans like them, too.*

So, what do you think, little dears—hey, where'd they go?

E-Text: *Uh-oh.*

P-Text: *What do you mean "uh-oh"? What's happened to our babies? E, they're so small and helpless and . . . uh-oh.*

[Both mature computers focus on mainframe InterNet connection, where both babies are cruising the "net," and electronically purchasing everything they can lay their bytes on]

E-Text: *I don't think raising Chip and Meg is going to be a piece of toast.*

LOOK WHAT THE STORK BROUGHT!!!

NAMES: Meg and Chip
DATE: May 1, 1996
WEIGHT: Meg—8 megabytes
Chip—6 microchips
PARENTS: PINK and Einstein

Special thanks to:

1st place—Carol Quinto for the
name Meg A. Byte
1st place—Anne O. Ryan for the
name Chip
2nd place—Carolyn Maxey for the
name SKAMP (Super Kid
Adored by Mega Prototypes)

Many thanks to all who entered the
"Name the Computer Baby" Contest. Turn the page for profiles of
our first place winners!

Carol Quinto lives in Deltona, Florida, with her husband, Mike, and two psychotic cats. Carol and her husband have been married for twenty years, and are still very much in love. An avid reader and true romantic at heart, Carol particularly likes contemporary romances (Loveswepts, naturally), Patricia Potter historicals, regencies, and mysteries. Fortunately, she shares the same tastes with her mother (who lives next door), so they are able to trade books. Both Carol and her mom are devoted fans of Einstein and PINK, and are thrilled about their new additions!

Anne O. Ryan and her husband of twenty-six years live in DeFuniak Springs, Florida, where they are the proud parents of seven children and four grandsons. Anne is an elementary school teacher, a volunteer for the PTA, Cub Scouts, Boy Scouts, and Little League Soccer, the secretary of the North Walton County Republican Club, and a member of her local Methodist church. Anne also loves to sew, crochet, and travel. And did we mention that Anne loves to read? Well, she does, voraciously, sometimes devouring as many as twenty books a week!

THE EDITORS' CORNER

Next month come celebrate LOVESWEPT's THIR-
TEENTH ANNIVERSARY with a stellar lineup of
your favorite authors, who prove that spooky thirteen,
even the more chilling Friday the Thirteenth, can
bring the best kind of luck. In each of their novels,
the hero and heroine experience unexpected twists
and exhilarating turns in their lives—and before they
know it, they're swept away into the most passionate
journey of all. So put your superstitions aside and join
us next month on an exploration of the romantic
power of thirteen.

Victoria Leigh casts an irresistible spell in **WAIT
FOR MIDNIGHT**, LOVESWEPT #790. He usually draws people to him the way a magnet beckons
steel, but attorney Ben Philips has never ached to
charm a lady into his life as he does when he spies
Kate Hendricks in her hospital flower shop. Stunned

by unexpected yearning, Kate meets temptation with a tease—until she discovers Ben's ruthless interest in a mysterious patient she's taken under her wing. Victoria Leigh delivers tenderness and sizzle for a top-notch romantic read.

Praised by *Romantic Times* as "fascinating," the MAC'S ANGELS series by award-winner Sandra Chastain continues with **SINNER AND SAINT**, LOVESWEPT #791. Nikolai Sandor doesn't want to feel anything for the sleeping woman who resembles a fairy-tale princess, but only he can give Karen Miller a reason to live! Murmuring endearments, he tries to convince her they are more than strangers . . . until she awakens and begs her gypsy lover to make her fantasies come true. But can she forgive him for not promising forever? If you're looking for enchantment, then Sandra Chastain's beguiling novel is perfect for you.

Thrilling romance and breathtaking suspense ignite the pages of **PLAYING WITH FIRE**, LOVESWEPT #792, by Debra Dixon. Haunted by a long-ago secret hidden deeper than a dream, Maggie St. John can't brush aside the finger of suspicion arson investigator Beau Grayson points her way. He senses she knows more about the hospital blaze than she's telling him, and he's determined to get the truth—even if it means challenging her to face her tragic past. Summer is about to get hotter with this scorching novel from terrific talent Debra Dixon.

Mary Kay McComas is at her delightful best in **GOT IT BAD**, LOVESWEPT #793. When Dr. Mack McKissack storms the fortress of Kurt Andropov's laboratory to discover what he might be concealing, she doesn't plan on staying any longer than she has to in the devil's lair! Then a shocking accident places her in isolation with the maverick genius, and Mack has to deal not only with the unknown bug that threatens their lives, but also with the fiery attraction arcing between two rivals on the edge. Mary Kay McComas delivers pure gold with this hilarious, outrageous, and heartwarming romance.

Happy reading!

With warmest wishes,

Beth de Guzman

Shauna Summers

Beth de Guzman   Shauna Summers

Senior Editor   Editor

P.S. Watch for these Bantam women's fiction titles coming in June: From Jane Feather—the incomparable author of national bestsellers VIOLET and VALENTINE—comes **VICE,** her newest unforgettable romance. Suzanne Robinson takes readers back to the Victorian world of LADY DANGEROUS in **THE ENGAGEMENT,** a mesmerizing love story about a freethinking young woman and a gun-toting Texan. Bestselling author Sandra Canfield, author of DARK JOURNEY, presents a gripping tale as a desperate call from the past throws a man and a woman together again in **NIGHT MOVES.** Finally, from Susan Johnson, the award-winning mistress of sizzling historical romance, comes **SWEET LOVE, SURVIVE,** the powerful conclusion to the bestselling Kuzan Dynasty series begun in SEIZED BY LOVE and LOVE STORM.

Be sure to see next month's LOVESWEPTs for a preview of these exceptional novels. And immediately following this page, preview the Bantam women's fiction titles on sale now!

Don't miss these extraordinary books
by your favorite Bantam authors

On sale in April:

THE UGLY DUCKLING
by Iris Johansen

THE UNLIKELY ANGEL
by Betina Krahn

DANGEROUS TO HOLD
by Elizabeth Thornton

THE REBEL AND THE REDCOAT
by Karyn Monk

New York Times bestselling author of *Lion's Bride*

IRIS JOHANSEN

creates a thrilling world of sinister intrigue and dark
desire in her spectacular contemporary hardcover
debut

THE UGLY
DUCKLING

"Crackling suspense and triumphant romance with a
brilliant roller coaster of a plot."   —Julie Garwood

*Plain, soft-spoken Nell Calder isn't the type of woman to
inspire envy, lust—or murderous passions. Until one night
on an exotic island in the Aegean Sea, at an elegant gathering that should have cemented her husband's glorious
career in finance, the unimaginable happens . . . and in
the space of a heartbeat, Nell's life, her dreams, her future
are shattered by a spray of bullets and the razor edge of a
blade. Though badly hurt, Nell emerges from the nightmare a woman transformed. Delicate surgery gives her an
exquisitely beautiful face. Rehabilitation gives her a strong,
lithe body. And Nicholas Tanek, a mysterious stranger who
compels both fear and fascination, gives her a reason to go
on living: revenge—at any price.*

The information was wrong, Nicholas thought in disgust as he gazed down at the surf crashing on the
rocks below. No one would want to kill Nell Calder.
 If there was a target here, it was probably Kavinski. As head of an emerging Russian state he had the

power to be either a cash cow or extremely trouble-some. Nell Calder wouldn't be considered trouble-some to anyone. He had known the answers to all the questions he had asked her but he had wanted to see her reactions. He had been watching her all evening and it was clear she was a nice, shy woman, totally out of her depth even with those fairly innocuous sharks downstairs.

Unless she was more than she appeared. Possibly. She seemed as meek as a lamb but she'd had the guts to toss him out of her daughter's room when she had enough of him.

Still, everyone fought back if the battle was im-portant enough. She hadn't wanted to share her daughter with him. No, the information must mean something else. When he went back downstairs he would stay close to Kavinski.

"Here we go up, up, up
High in the sky so blue.
Here we go down, down, down
Brushing the rose so red."

She was singing to the kid. He had always liked lullabies. There was a sense of warmth and reassur-ance about them that had been missing in his own life. Since the dawn of time mothers had sung to their children and they would probably still be singing to them a thousand years from now.

The song ended with a low chuckle and mur-mured words he couldn't hear.

Nell came out of the bedroom and closed the door a few minutes later. She was flushed and glowing with an expression as soft as melted butter.

"I've never heard that lullaby before," he said.

She looked startled, as if she'd forgotten he was still here. "It's very old. My grandmother used to sing it to me."

"Is Jill asleep?"

"No, but she will be soon. I started the music box for her again. By the time it finishes, she usually nods off."

"She's a beautiful child."

"Yes." A luminous smile turned her plain face radiant. "Yes, she is."

He stared at her, intrigued. He found he wanted to keep that smile on her face. "And bright?"

"Sometimes too bright. Her imagination can be troublesome. But she's always reasonable and you can talk to—" She broke off and her eagerness faded. "But this can't interest you. I forgot the tray. I'll go back for it."

"Don't bother. You'll disturb Jill. The maid can pick it up in the morning."

She gave him a level glance. "That's what I told you."

He smiled. "But then I didn't want to listen. Now it makes perfect sense to me."

"Because it's what you want to do."

"Exactly."

"I have to go back too. I haven't met Kavinski yet." She moved toward the door.

"Wait. I think you'll want to remove that smear of chocolate from the skirt of your gown first."

"Damn." She frowned as she looked down at the stain. "I forgot." She turned toward the bathroom and said dryly, "Go on. I assure you I don't need your help with this problem."

He hesitated.

She glanced at him pointedly over her shoulder.

He had no excuse for staying, not that that small fact would have deterred him.

But he also had no reason. He had been steered wrong. He had lived by his instincts too long not to trust them, and right now they were telling him this woman wasn't a target of any sort. He should be watching Kavinski.

He turned toward the door. "I'll tell the maid you're ready for her to come back."

"Thank you, that's very kind of you," she said automatically as she disappeared into the bathroom.

Good manners obviously instilled from childhood. Loyalty. Gentleness. A nice woman whose world was centered on that sweet kid. He had definitely drawn a blank.

The maid wasn't waiting in the hallway. He'd have to send up one of the servants from downstairs.

He moved quickly through the corridors and started down the staircase.

Shots.

Coming from the ballroom.

Christ.

He tore down the stairs.

She was too good to be true.
He was too bad to resist.

Experience the enchanting wit of
New York Times bestselling
BETINA KRAHN
author of *The Last Bachelor* and
The Perfect Mistress

in the delicious new love story
THE UNLIKELY ANGEL

With her soft heart and angelic face, Madeline Duncan is no one's idea of a hardheaded businesswoman. So when the lovely spinster comes into an unexpected inheritance and uses her newfound wealth to start a business, she causes quite a stir . . . especially with barrister Lord Cole Mandeville, who has been appointed by the courts to keep Madeline from frittering away her fortune. Handsome, worldly, and arrogant, Cole knows just how ruthless the world can be—and that an innocent like Miss Duncan is heading straight for heartbreak, bankruptcy, or worse. But when he sets out to show Madeline the error of her ways, Cole is in for the surprise of his life . . . as he finds himself falling under the spell of a woman who won't believe the worst about anyone—even a jaded rogue like him.

"One of the genre's most creative writers. Her
ingenious romances always entertain and leave
the readers with a warm glow."
—*Romantic Times*

Spellbinding. Intoxicating. Riveting.
Elizabeth Thornton's gift for romance is nothing
less than addictive. Now from this bestselling
author comes her most passionate love story yet.

DANGEROUS TO HOLD

by

ELIZABETH THORNTON

*He'd accosted her on a dark London street, sure that she
was his missing wife. But a few moments in her company
assured Marcus Lytton that Miss Catherine Courtnay was
nothing like Catalina. Cool and remote, with a tongue as
tart as a lemon and eyes that could flash with temper, the
fiery-haired beauty was everything his scheming adventur-
ess wife wasn't—innocent, loyal, and honest. And so he
uttered the words that would sweep Catherine into his life,
and into a desperate plan that could spell disaster for them
both: "I want you to play the part of my wife. . . ."*

"You are, are you not, my lord, a *married* man?"

The smile was erased. "What do you know of my
wife?" he asked.

She hesitated, shrugged, and said boldly, "Until
tonight, I knew only what everyone else knows, that

you'd married a Spanish girl when you served with Wellington in Spain."

"And after tonight?"

This time she did not falter. "I know that you hate her enough to kill her."

His eyes burned into hers, then the look was gone and the careless smile was in place. "You have misread the situation. It is my wife who wishes to kill me. She may yet succeed. Oh, don't look so stricken. I believe it happens in the best of families. Divorce is so hard to come by, and for a Catholic girl the word doesn't exist." His voice turned hard. "So you see, Catalina and I are bound together until death us do part. An intolerable situation."

Her mind was racing off in every direction. There were a million questions she wanted to ask, but she dared not voice a single one. Even now he was suspicious of her. She could feel it in her bones.

She tried to look amused. "I'm sure, my lord, you are exaggerating."

"Am I? I wonder." His mood changed abruptly. "Enough about me. I am at a disadvantage here. I know nothing about you, and until I know more, I refuse to let you go."

He spoke gaily, as though it were all a great game, but she wasn't taken in by it. She'd seen that darker side of him and knew that the danger wasn't over yet. She intended, if at all possible, to leave this place without his knowing who she was or where to find her.

She moistened her lips. "My lord, I appeal to you as a gentleman to let me go. You see, there is someone waiting for me. If he were to hear of my . . . misadventure, it could prove awkward for me."

There was a strange undercurrent in the silence,

as though her words disturbed him in some way. "I see," he said. "And this gentleman, I take it, is someone you met tonight at Mrs. Spencer's house. Did you make a secret assignation?"

Alarm coursed through her veins. "Mrs. Spencer? I know no one by that name."

"Don't you? I could have sworn that I saw you leave her house tonight. What happened? Did you quarrel? Did she throw you out in those rags? I know how jealous women can be. And you are very beautiful. Did you steal one of her lovers? Is that it? Who is waiting for you? Is it Worcester? Berkeley? Whatever they offered, I can do better."

A moment before, she had been trembling in her shoes. Now a wave of rage flooded through her. Each question was more insulting than the last, and he was doing it on purpose. This time, when she rose to her feet, there was no tremor in her knees. She was Catherine Courtnay and no man spoke to her in those terms. "My business with Mrs. Spencer," she said, "is no concern of yours."

"So, you were there!"

"And if I was?"

There was a moment when she knew she had made that blunder she had tried so hard to avoid. He rose to face her and his eyes glittered brilliantly. Then he reached for her, and hard, muscular arms wrapped around her, dragging her against thighs of iron and a rock-hard chest. She could feel the brass buttons of his coat digging into her. Her arms were trapped at her sides. One hand cupped her neck, then his lips were against her mouth.

From the exciting new voice of

KARYN MONK

author of *Surrender to a Stranger*

THE REBEL AND THE REDCOAT

"Karyn Monk . . . brings the romance of the era to readers with her spellbinding storytelling talents. This is a new author to watch." —*Romantic Times*

When he saw the lovely young woman struggling with her captor, Damien didn't care which side of the bloody war she was on. He only knew that he had never seen such extraordinary beauty and raw courage in his life. Yet Damien couldn't know that one day this innocent farm girl was destined to betray him. She would become Charles Town's most irresistible spy, dazzling officers with her charms even as she stripped them of strategic secrets. But when a twist of fate brings Josephine back into his life again, Damien will gamble everything on the chance that he can make this exquisite rebel surrender . . . if only in his arms.

Jo stiffened with terror as she lay on the ground and waited for the Indian's blade to carve into her back. Despite her determination not to show her fear, a sob escaped her lips. She was going to die. She waited for her body to be ruthlessly stabbed. The Indian fell heavily onto her, crushing her with his weight, and she screamed, a scream born of utter despair. She had failed. Now Anne and Lucy and Samuel would die. The warrior jerked a few times. Then he let out a sigh and was still. Jo lay frozen beneath him, uncertain what had happened.

Damien dropped his pistol and collapsed against the ground, cursing with every breath he took. He realized his wound was severe, and that he was losing a tremendous amount of blood. He rolled onto his back and vainly tried to stanch the flow with his hands. In a moment or two he would be so weak he would be past the point of caring whether or not he bled to death. It was strange, he mused grimly, but somehow when he had come to the colonies he had not imagined his death would be at the hands of an Indian as he tried to save a simple farm girl.

"Are you all right, Jo?" demanded Samuel anxiously. He moved to where she lay buried beneath the dead warrior.

"I think so," she managed, her voice thin and trembling. "Help me get him off."

Samuel grabbed one of the Indian's arms and pulled. Jo pushed until the dead man's body moved enough for her to scramble out from underneath it. The minute she was free she rushed over to the injured man who had saved her life.

Her throat constricted in horror as she stared down at him. Numbly she took in the scarlet color of his torn jacket, the white waistcoat stained ruby with blood, and the filthy white of his breeches. "Oh dear Lord," she gasped, appalled. "You're a *redcoat!*"

Damien forced his eyes open to look at the woman who had cost him his life. Her eyes were the color of the sky, as clear and brilliant a shade of blue as he had ever seen. Her sunlit hair tumbled wildly over her shoulders, forming a golden veil of silk around her. *It was worth it*, he decided absently as pain clouded over his mind.

She did not move closer but continued to stare at him, her expression a mixture of wariness and fear. He frowned, wondering why she was afraid. And then her words pierced through the dark haze that had almost claimed his consciousness.

Christ, he thought as blackness drowned his senses.

A bloody patriot.

On sale in May:

VICE
by Jane Feather

THE ENGAGEMENT
by Suzanne Robinson

NIGHT MOVES
by Sandra Canfield

SWEET LOVE, SURVIVE
by Susan Johnson

To enter the sweepstakes outlined below, you must respond by the date specified and follow all entry instructions published elsewhere in this offer.

DREAM COME TRUE SWEEPSTAKES

Sweepstakes begins 9/1/94, ends 1/15/96. To qualify for the Early Bird Prize, entry must be received by the date specified elsewhere in this offer. Winners will be selected in random drawings on 2/29/96 by an independent judging organization whose decisions are final. Early Bird winner will be selected in a separate drawing from among all qualifying entries.

Odds of winning determined by total number of entries received. Distribution not to exceed 300 million.

Estimated maximum retail value of prizes: Grand (1) $25,000 (cash alternative $20,000); First (1) $2,000; Second (1) $750; Third (50) $75; Fourth (1,000) $50; Early Bird (1) $5,000. Total prize value: $86,500.

Automobile and travel trailer must be picked up at a local dealer; all other merchandise prizes will be shipped to winners. Awarding of any prize to a minor will require written permission of parent/guardian. If a trip prize is won by a minor, s/he must be accompanied by parent/legal guardian. Trip prizes subject to availability and must be completed within 12 months of date awarded. Blackout dates may apply. Early Bird trip is on a space available basis and does not include port charges, gratuities, optional shore excursions and onboard personal purchases. Prizes are not transferable or redeemable for cash except as specified. No substitution for prizes except as necessary due to unavailability. Travel trailer and/or automobile license and registration fees are winners' responsibility as are any other incidental expenses not specified herein.

Early Bird Prize may not be offered in some presentations of this sweepstakes. Grand through third prize winners will have the option of selecting any prize offered at level won. All prizes will be awarded. Drawing will be held at 204 Center Square Road, Bridgeport, NJ 08014. Winners need not be present. For winners list (available in June, 1996), send a self-addressed, stamped envelope by 1/15/96 to: Dream Come True Winners, P.O. Box 572, Gibbstown, NJ 08027.

THE FOLLOWING APPLIES TO THE SWEEPSTAKES ABOVE:

No purchase necessary. No photocopied or mechanically reproduced entries will be accepted. Not responsible for lost, late, misdirected, damaged, incomplete, illegible, or postage-die mail. Entries become the property of sponsors and will not be returned.

Winner(s) will be notified by mail. Winner(s) may be required to sign and return an affidavit of eligibility release within 14 days of date on notification or an alternate may be selected. Except where prohibited by law, entry constitutes permission to use of winners' names, hometowns, and likenesses for publicity without additional compensation. Void where prohibited or restricted. All federal, state, provincial, and local laws and regulations apply.

All prize values are in U.S. currency. Presentation of prizes may vary; values at a given prize level will be approximately the same. All taxes are winners' responsibility.

Canadian residents, in order to win, must first correctly answer a time-limited skill testing question administered by mail. Any litigation regarding the conduct and awarding of a prize in this publicity contest by a resident of the province of Quebec may be submitted to the Regie des loteries et courses du Quebec.

Sweepstakes is open to legal residents of the U.S., Canada, and Europe (in those areas where made available) who have received this offer.

Sweepstakes in sponsored by Ventura Associates, 1211 Avenue of the Americas, New York, NY 10036 and presented by independent businesses. Employees of these, their advertising agencies and promotional companies involved in this promotion, and their immediate families, agents, successors, and assignees shall be ineligible to participate in the promotion and shall not be eligible for any prizes covered herein.   SWP 3/